The Fifth Beethoven

Melanie Jackson

The Fifth Beethoven

Melanie Jackson

CₑP | CRWTH PRESS

Library and Archives Canada Cataloguing in Publication

Title: The fifth Beethoven / Melanie Jackson.
Names: Jackson, Melanie, 1956- author.
Identifiers: Canadiana (print) 20200264400 | Canadiana (eb-
ook) 20200265423 | ISBN 9781989724057
(softcover) | ISBN 9781989724064 (EPUB)
Classification: LCC PS8569.A265 F54 2020 | DDC jC813/.6—dc23

Cover illustration by Matej Beg
Cover and interior design by Julia Breese
Copy edited by Renée Layberry
Proofread by Audrey McClennan

Published by
Crwth Press
#204 – 2320 Woodland Drive
Vancouver, BC V5N 3P2
778-302-5525

Printed and bound in Canada on 100% post-consumer waste (PCW) paper.

23 22 21 20 · 4 3 2 1

To my Vancouver Symphony
Orchestra date, Bart Jackson.

Also to my brother Greg—and the staff at
Kerry's Place Autism Services, Ontario,
for their big hearts and all that they do.

Overture

The news vendor thumped the morning papers down in front of his kiosk. He glanced at the headline: *Random purse, wallet thefts on the rise, police warn.*

The vendor sighed. Another day, another depressing story. Which he wouldn't read. The vendor didn't want depressing. What he wanted was his morning coffee. He had it ready in his hand, double cream, double sugar.

A shadow fell on the newspapers. First customer.

Or maybe not. This was a read-and-run type, the vendor decided. So many people were like that. Too cheap to buy.

The vendor's dream was to sell flowers. Tulips were his favourite. Tulips of all kinds and colours. Striped tulips. Big tulips. Tiny tulips. He grew tulips at home, on his south-facing balcony. One day he'd save enough to open—oh, not a shop. In Vancouver, the rent would be way too high. He'd still be a sidewalk vendor, only with flowers.

Peeling the lid off his coffee, the vendor pictured a kiosk overflowing with blossoms, a splash of brilliance and fragrance amid the soaring steel towers of downtown. He'd have discerning customers as opposed to the ill-mannered ones he too often served now. The read-and-runs. With a flower kiosk the vendor would be free of them. He sipped his double-double coffee and dreamed on.

Pop! Pop! Pop!

Startled, the vendor spilled coffee down the *Vancouver Sun* T-shirt the newspaper paid him to wear. (Every little bit helped.) Gross. Read-And-Run was cracking all ten knuckles.

"Maybe you could do that somewhere else," the vendor snapped.

Read-And-Run shoved a five-dollar bill into his hand, grabbed a newspaper and marched off.

"Hey! Don't you want your change?"

Read-And-Run just kept going.

The vendor shook his head. Some people. Maybe he'd head back to the coffee place and ask for a third cream and sugar.

One thing he definitely knew: he was keeping Read-And-Run's change.

After all, every little bit helped.

Chapter One

It was a longer note than any I'd ever played.

I stood, head tipped back, gawking up at it. If you were like me and into music, the sight of Vancouver's newest luxury building, the Keynote, was an instant—well, high. The Keynote stretched 600 feet up in a design that was pure melody. Pure quarter note, to be exact. At its base, forming the notehead, the Keynote had a black oval-shaped lobby. The tall black-glass tower was the stem. From the top, glittery silver in the shape of a quarter-note flag stretched down several stories.

The tower's black glass reflected sun, clouds and other towers in Coal Harbour, a posh section of downtown. People used to notice the bright, tilting Trump tower down the block. Not anymore. Now the Keynote was the architectural melody they lingered on.

In TV commercials, Keynote builder Mike Dante explained his choice of design: "Life should be music!" I liked that. I liked also that he'd used an award-winning, international architect with a musical name: Renzo—wait for it—*Piccolo*.

Sure, I knew the life/music line was a sales pitch. Mike Dante wanted people to buy office and condo space in the Keynote. And they did. The place sold out. With his twinkling eyes and big smile, Mike Dante was an expert salesperson. You couldn't blow a gum bubble in Vancouver without it sticking to a Dante development.

Sales pitch or not, the Keynote was cool. Just looking at it made my fingers itch for piano keys. Not that this was unusual. Gazing up at the Keynote now, I started snapping my fingers.

"Planning to *scale* the Keynote?"

The voice belonged to a guy dressed up

like Ludwig van Beethoven: frilly shirt, black pants, messy black wig, mask with jutting cheekbones and thick, scowling eyebrows.

He offered me a brochure. *The Keynote restaurant, Andante, opens soon! Book it for your wedding, your family reunion, your birthday party.*

The Andante. I liked the wordplay on the owner's name. Plus, in music *andante* meant easygoing, no fuss, no stress. A cool name for a resto. But me, a fifteen-year-old Charlie's Chicken dishwasher, book at the Andante? I laughed. "Not on my salary."

"Always think on a positive note!" he said as he moved on.

The real Beethoven—the German-born Beethoven (1770–1827)—was my personal inspiration. When Mom started teaching me piano, I found it tough. It was a lot to remember all at once and a lot to practise. I got impatient. Which was my common reaction to life. I mean, impatience is so instantly satisfying.

One day after I complained, Mom said, "Think this is hard? For much of his life

Beethoven was deaf!" I never forgot that. If Beethoven could compose without hearing, I guessed I could handle sharps, flats and scales.

Mom told me something else about Beethoven. Like me, he'd been impatient. He dedicated his *Third Symphony* to the French general, Napoleon Bonaparte. But then the general got power-hungry and made himself emperor. Furious and disillusioned, Beethoven ripped up the dedication page. An impulsive type of guy. I could identify with that.

Beethoven's *Fifth Symphony* thrummed into my head now. I had the short, easy-sheet-music version down solid. I'd been thinking I should try the real version.

"Bah-bah-bah-*boom…* bah-bah-bah-*boom*," I sang softly. Nothing rocked like the first four notes of the *Fifth*.

Someone crashed into my right shoulder. I staggered sideways, almost fell. Straightened up with fists ready. Whoever had tackled me, I was ready to return the favour.

The Fifth Beethoven

The sun was at his back. I could hardly see him. But his unruly-wigged head gave him away. The guy in the Beethoven outfit. He ducked like he knew I might try to punch him. Lifting his right hand from a pocket he wiped away a pretend tear.

I guessed this was Fake Beethoven for *I'm sorry*. I pushed my hair back off my forehead, a habit I have when exasperated. I get exasperated easily, so my hair has a wild, uncombed look. Unruly hair. Something else I have in common with the late Ludwig.

"You should be more careful," I told Fake Beethoven. "I was tempted to help myself to a fistful of mask."

He placed his right hand over his left and squeezed. *Pop, pop, pop!* Then, left hand over right, he blasted out an encore. If knuckle-cracking was an Olympic sport, Fake Beethoven would clean up on gold.

He turned and jogged across the Keynote courtyard. As usual, the courtyard was crowded. Locals and tourists showed up all day, every day to stare at the Keynote. Most oohed over it. Some complained about the design, saying that a building should look like a building.

Then there were the protesters. They held up cardboard signs showing Mike Dante's face with a big X over it. Shouted, "Give us back our homes!"

Fake Beethoven zigzagged through the crowd. Near the Keynote entrance he collided with a girl my age. They both hit the ground. He grabbed the arm of a nearby woman, pulled himself up. The woman was wearing stiletto heels. Not great for balance. Down she went, too.

By now everyone was watching. Some laughed, thinking it was a comedy routine.

Fake Beethoven ran off, waving. Not just waving his hand, though. He was waving the girl's cloth bag and the woman's purse.

He ran into the Keynote's lobby and disappeared.

I had a sudden, sick feeling. I clapped a hand against my back pocket.

My wallet was gone. With it, the two one-hundred dollar bills I'd cashed from my latest Charlie's Chicken paycheck. I had plans for that money. My local music store on Commercial Drive had second-hand noise-isolating headphones set aside for me. Bose headphones, the best of the best. I'd been wanting some for ages. Once I plugged the Bose into our electric piano at home, I would only hear my playing. No shrill cackles piercing up through the floor from our landlady. No audience screams from the reality shows our neighbour beside us watched. No car alarms from the street. Nothing.

But now that wouldn't happen. Bye-bye, Bose.

I remembered Fake Beethoven raising one hand from a pocket to wipe away a pretend tear. Now I understood. The moment before, he'd slipped my wallet into the pocket.

People were helping the girl and woman up. The girl winced. She was having trouble standing. The woman started screaming.

"My jewels! My *jewels!*" Bystanders jabbed at cellphones, calling 911.

I wasn't in the mood to wait for police. Like Beethoven, I was impulsive. And I had a score to settle.

I charged over to the Keynote lobby. I yanked open one of the black-glass doors, looked around the lobby—and spotted him.

Except it was the real Beethoven, glowering at me from a big portrait. I nodded at him in greeting. One wild-haired, impatient guy to another.

On a black door in a curving glass wall, the word *Andante* sparkled in silver letters. I tried the door. Locked. Flattening my nose against the glass I squinted inside.

No costumed composer. No anybody. The restaurant wasn't open to the public yet. There weren't even tables and chairs. Just a long, sleek black bar and—whoa. I gaped. A grand piano. What a beauty.

Enough sightseeing. I had a thief to catch. I looked around some more. He had to be here somewhere. I walked along the curving restaurant. Any second I might come upon him, chuckling as he counted his stolen loot.

A plaque gleamed at me from the wall:

BUSINESS PERSON OF
THE YEAR AWARD

THE CITY OF VANCOUVER COMMENDS MIKE DANTE

FOR FINDING NEW HOMES — NEW BEGINNINGS —

FOR ALL THOSE DISPLACED BY HIS DEVELOPMENTS.

I didn't get it. If Mike Dante had found homes for everyone, why the protests? Talk about a wrong note.

But wondering about that wasn't going to help find the thief and my money. I followed the curving glass wall and came to a door. *Employees Only*. Like that was going to stop me. I twisted the knob.

The door opened into the Andante. Across the shiny black floor, past the grand piano, sunshine flooded in. The floor-to-ceiling glass doors stood open.

That's how the thief had escaped.

I walked over and looked out at the people milling around, gazing up, snapping photos. No Fake Beethoven. By now he'd probably pulled off his wig and mask. Blended into the crowd.

On the top of the piano, with my palms, I beat out this thought: *Goodbye, two hundred dollars*.

My eyes went to the closed fallboard. I walked slowly around to it. To me an unused piano was like unused oxygen. I raised the fallboard, ran a finger down the keys. The thought of my stolen wallet faded. I was here, alone with a grand piano that needed to be played.

I found G, the first note of the *Fifth Symphony*. Lightly I pressed G, G, G, E-flat. The famous beginning, the bah-bah-bah-boom. Me, a home-taught improviser of music, playing a grand. I felt like I was in a dream.

I poised my hands over the keys. Taking a deep breath I plunged them, played bah-bah-bah-*bo-o-oom*! This was more like it.

No. Not more like it. This *was* it. Music

was everything to me. I started jumping around, like I did playing at home. With one difference. At home my feet hit the floor. Here, after a few jumps, they landed on—

Shoes. I stopped playing, looked down. Shiny black leather shoes.

Bah-bah-bah—uh-oh.

I stepped off the shoes. Their owner, a burly guy with the words *Keynote Security* on his shirt, glared at me. He clamped a hand on my shoulder. A big hand. A big wrist, too. The band of his smart watch strained around it, stretched thin and ready to snap.

I tried the friendly approach. "Nice watch-band. You can't beat basic gray."

The guard tightened his hold on my shoulder. He snarled, "Trespassing is a crime. You're busted, moron."

I heard splintering sounds. Those would be my shoulder bones, crumbling in his grip.

Chapter Two

"Let him go."

The voice was amused. But the effect was instant. The security guard's hand flew up like my shoulder was radioactive.

The splintering noises continued. I turned around. Not bones breaking—ice cubes clinking. A man was holding a glass of water under an ice dispenser. He brought the glass to me.

I recognized the curly blond hair, the sunny smile, the bright blue eyes from TV commercials. My throat went dry as I choked out, "M-Mr. Dante."

What had I been thinking, bashing out Beethoven's *Fifth* on his grand piano? The grand was out of my league. This whole place was out of my league.

"Sorry," I gulped. "I was just—I was angry when I came in. I'd had my wallet stolen."

Mike Dante's bright gaze fixed on me. "And playing music was your way of dealing with it."

I thought about this. About how every day at Charlie's Chicken I'd scrape food, even chewed-gum wads, off customers' plates. Then I'd go home, play piano and forget.

I said slowly, "Music makes stuff go away. Or at least parks it in a corner. I play whenever I can. The louder, the better."

He nodded like he understood. "Royal Conservatory of Music?"

Nervousness made me stupid. "Don't know that tune. Wait—I mean…"

Mr. Dante roared with laughter. "A funny piano player. I like that."

He took a roll of bills from his pocket. "How much got stolen?"

I gaped. I'd never seen a roll that fat. If Mr. Dante ran out of things to buy he could use it to plug leaks.

"Two hundred," I replied. "I'd just cashed my pay."

The Keynote owner began peeling off bills. "What's your name, piano player? And call me Mike."

I was too dazzled to think. My name. I could do this. "Nate Crocker. But I can't take your money. It's not right."

"Sure it is. You got robbed on my property. And what is your job, Nate?" Mr. Dante—Mike—pressed a hundred-dollar bill and five twenties into my hand.

I hesitated. Saying *dishwasher* would sound lame. I wanted to impress this guy. I'd never met a tycoon before.

I made my face worried and thoughtful, the look I'd seen on executives lining up for Charlie's Chicken lunches-to-go. I imagined how Mike would introduce himself. *I'm in real estate.*

I cleared my throat. "I'm in soap."

That set him off laughing again. Too late I remembered I was wearing my Charlie's Chicken apron. Not exactly your up-and-coming CEO image. But Mike Dante's laugh was infectious. Even feeling like an idiot, I grinned.

"Let me ask you something," Mike said, when he'd recovered. "How would you like to work for me? Take your hands out of soap suds and put them on piano keys?"

From Mike's penthouse office I looked across sunlit harbour to the blue coastal mountains. Seagulls skimmed past, shrieking. They soared over sailboats and freighters, then out to sea. They kept going, kept chasing the sun.

Mike sat back in his leather chair. He waited while I gazed out some more. While I made sure I was really here, hadn't imagined him inviting me up. When I finally sat down on the other side of his desk, he studied me. "What do you want out of life, Nate Crocker?"

Guidance counsellors asked me that and I shrugged. What I wanted wasn't in a career-planning manual.

"I want to be like you," I said. "On top of

the world. And like those gulls, making a lot of noise while I'm at it."I thought he'd laugh again. But he looked pleased. "I like people with dreams. Determined dreamers like you. You saw a grand piano and you had to play it. Forget rules about trespassing. You believe in yourself and you break rules."

I stared. He got that rule-breaking was what music was all about. Beethoven outraged critics when he included a part for singers in his "Ode to Joy." All great composers break rules. That's what makes them great.

Mike smiled. "I've surprised you. But that's how I built Dante Enterprises. You play Beethoven in the key of rock? I play business in the key of surprise."

I liked the way Mike talked to me. Like he trusted me. No wonder he was success-ful. He made you comfortable. Made you trust him.

Mike snapped his fingers and pointed at me. "That's why I'm giving you a start on what you want out of life. You'll play piano outside, eleven to two. Rock the courtyard."

The Fifth Beethoven

I couldn't believe it. I had an urge to swivel, see the person behind me he was talking to.

He said, "Right now people stop, stare, move on. Soon I'll be opening the Andante restaurant. I want them to get in the habit of stopping and *staying*. With you on piano, they'll do that—now and when the restaurant is up and running. You'll be the lunchtime entertainment. They won't want to think about anything else. Won't want to leave."

This was really happening. He was offering me a gig. A music gig. *Me*.

"Wow," I breathed.

"Think you can handle it?"

Oh, man. I'd have to practise like crazy. Improve my playing on the songs I knew, learn new ones. And even then I'd still be what I was now, a total amateur. Me, handle a gig? Of course not.

"Of course I can handle it," I said.

"Excellent. A new beginning for you. Because I believe in new beginnings. You've heard of Seneca?"

"A new band?"

Mike laughed. "Seneca was an ancient Roman. He said: *Every new beginning comes from some other beginning's end*. It's my motto. An end shouldn't mean *the* end. It should mean a fresh beginning."

I thought of the plaque in the lobby. The Businessperson of the Year Award. I said, "Like the people who used to live in the apartment buildings here. You helped them find new homes."

Mike beamed. "Exactly! We understand each other. I see a long, prosperous business relationship for us."

For us, I thought. *Us*. Tycoon Mike and nobody me. Bah-bah-bah-*boom*.

Mike's desk phone beeped. He pressed a button on it.

"Your son is here," a voice chirped.

"Send him in!"

Fake Beethoven strolled into the room.

Forget the key of surprise. This was the key of earthquake-level shock.

"Yo, Dad." Fake Beethoven pushed his mask up on top of his wig so it sat like a hat. With a wave at me he flopped down on the sofa at the far end of the room and closed his eyes.

"You're—you're—" *the thief*, I wanted to blurt. But I was conflicted. Mike had just given me my break into show business. Tossing accusations at his kid seemed harsh.

Mike called out introductions. "Nate Crocker, Bo Dante. Nate's going to work for us, Bo. Play piano in the courtyard."

"Cool," mumbled Bo.

I relaxed. I couldn't see this guy being the thief. It took energy to barrel through a crowd grabbing purses and wallets. Bo Dante looked like he'd barely be able to crack open a book.

Bo had been the easygoing, jokey Beethoven I'd met earlier. I recognized his voice. That is to say, he'd been the first Beethoven. Which meant…

I turned back to Mike, speaking in a low voice so as not to wake Sleeping Bo-ty. "We have a Beethoven problem. As in more than one wigged, masked composer. The person who stole my wallet was wearing the same costume."

Mike tapped his phone and nodded. "My security guy just texted me. The police are in the courtyard, talking to witnesses." He shook his head. "What a world, huh? I hire a few Beethovens to hand out brochures, make jokes. Some bozo wears the same costume and rips off wallets. Unbelievable."

He had a sad, faraway expression. Mom got that sometimes, too. It was an adult thing.

"Earth to—I mean, excuse me, Mike. You said you'd hired a *few* Beethovens?"

He brightened. "Yeah. Bo and two of his buddies. They take turns working the courtyard."

Three Beethovens. In my mind they surrounded me, scowling. I wondered how to put my next question diplomatically. "Doesn't that mean one of them—not your son, of course—is the...er..."

"The thief?" Mike's eyes twinkled. He pressed a button on his office phone. "Ms. Laharne, where were my three Beethovens during the past hour? Up to something criminal, would you say?"

A whinnying giggle pealed through the speaker. "Only in the amount of pizza they ate. Pruitt took them to lunch, as usual."

Pruitt. Sounded like a butler. I had a new thought and clutched my hair. "Noooo."

Mike laughed. "What, you're worried about their calorie intake?"

"Not calories, Mike. Beethovens. Counting the thief, this means there's a *fourth* one."

Through the speaker, Ms. Laharne interrupted us. This time she didn't whinny-giggle. "Constable Barker to see you, Mr. Dante."

The door opened. A stony-faced policeman walked in.

Mike stood. His smile disappeared. "This is Nate Crocker, officer. He's the guy you're looking for."

And I realized: the job offer was a setup. I'd trespassed. Mike had tricked me into coming up here so the police could nab me.

Chapter Three

Visions of jail cells crowded my brain. "It was an impulse...I didn't mean..."

Mike held his frown a moment longer, then howled with laughter. "Just messing with you, kid. I joke around a lot, y'know?" He winked. "I'm like you. I like to entertain."

His voice turned businesslike. "Constable Barker is here to ask you about the robbery. Constable, Nate is a promising new employee of Dante Enterprises. You can talk in the conference room. You want coffee, food, just ask my assistant, Ms. Laharne. She takes care of everything."

Ms. Laharne was pale, slight and middle-aged, with straw-blonde hair. She was also the whinnying giggler, as I found out when she walked the constable and me to the conference room. As well as whinnying, she batted her eyes at the tall constable. "Oh, a policeman! How exciting."

The constable and I settled into chairs at a long table. It was black marble, so well-polished I could see my big smile in it. *A promising new employee*. Man, I was going places.

Ms. Laharne gave me an encouraging smile. For someone who whinnied, she was okay. She shut the conference room door to give us privacy.

Constable Barker took out his phone and poised his thumbs over it. "I have statements from the other two victims. Tell me about your experience."

I described looking up at the Keynote. Getting distracted with thoughts of music. The thief slamming into me, pretending it was an accident. His slam 2.0 into the girl, then the lady in high heels. Making off with the woman's purse and the girl's bag. The knock-the-oxygen-out-of-me feeling when I realized he'd also taken my wallet.

"There's one other thing," I said, as the constable tap-tapped. "The thief—the fourth Beethoven—has a nervous tic. He cracks his knuckles. Loudly." To illustrate I tried cracking my own knuckles. Nothing happened. I guessed knuckle-cracking was like piano. It took dedication and practice.

Wait. Maybe I could simulate the sound. I pressed my lips together, then *popped!* them open. I repeated this a few times.

I thought my sound effects were impressive. The constable just kept tapping notes into his phone. "How tall was the thief?"

I hesitated. The thief had moved fast. And the sun had been behind him. True, he'd stopped to wipe away a pretend tear and to knuckle-crack. But he'd been hunched, not standing straight. "Average height. I *think*."

Tap, tap. "What did the thief take?"

"A wallet that had about two hundred dollars in it. And a customer loyalty card. Let's just say I won't be getting a free tenth doughnut anytime soon."

That got a chuckle out of the constable. Except I wasn't joking. I'd been looking forward to double-glazed chocolate sprinkled with walnuts.

"Can you confirm I got this right?" The constable handed me his phone.

My name plus my stolen items sat on one line. I noticed the lines above, with two other names and lists of items: *Susan Volker: lipstick, cellphone, heirloom ruby earrings she was taking in for repair, Hermès scarf.*

Susan would be the middle-aged woman who'd screamed. I didn't blame her. The thief took her jewelry. And I didn't know what Hermès was, but just the accent told me the scarf was expensive.

I read about the other victim, the girl my age. *Zandi Singh: cellphone, Give Us Back Our Homes! file, half-eaten bag of baby carrots.* So Zandi was one of the protesters.

"Planning to do a book report on that?" Barker asked.

"Er, sorry." I handed the phone back. "I was just curious. The fourth Beethoven sure lucked out with the rubies."

He nodded. "There's been a rash of random purse and wallet snatchings.

Happens every tourist season. People walk around basking in the sunshine, admiring the scenery—and making themselves easy targets. Though this is the first time we've had a thief disguised as Beethoven."

"I guess it's like playing the lottery," I mused. "You get jewelry from one person, carrots from another."

The thief would toss the carrots, I decided. But he would enjoy that free doughnut. And he would probably never be caught. Unless by chance one day I happened to meet someone with that same nervous, knuckle-cracking tic…

Constable Barker was watching me curiously. "Anything to add?"

"Just…" I pressed my lips together. *Pop! Pop! Pop!*

"Mike Dante, *the* Mike Dante, hiring you just like that? It seems too good to be true." Mom gazed anxiously across our kitchen table at me as if I had a fever.

"It's good and it's true, Mom. Believe it." I speared a piece of broccoli. That was the easy part. Eating it was another matter. "Mike believes in me, Mom. I told him about how playing music makes stuff go away. And he *got* it. He's cool. He's—"

I realized I couldn't speak. In my excitement I'd put the broccoli into my mouth. That's what a big break in show biz will do. Distract you from your food enemies.

Mom still looked anxious. "What about Charlie's Chicken? You said they liked you. The boss was going to train you as a server. Like Chester."

Yee-ouch. The topic of my long-time buddy Chester was a sore point, one I preferred not to think about. Chester had got me the job at Charlie's Chicken. I'd pleaded, begged, nagged him to recommend me. Like most kids I knew, for me summer was a chance to earn in a high-cost city where our parents couldn't afford big allowances. You'd take any job, you didn't care what.

When I quit Charlie's Chicken and explained that I couldn't give the regulation two weeks' notice because I had to practise, the manager got mad. His mad I could take. My buddy's mad was tougher.

I was still trying to apologize. Before dinner, I'd phoned Ches. *Hi, it's me, your friendly neighbourhood ingrate. Listen, sorry about—*

Click! End of call. Possibly the end of a long buddyship. Fine. Regrets and guilt weren't productive. So I wouldn't bother with them, wouldn't think about letting Ches and Charlie's Chicken down.

Mom was watching me with that unnerving see-into-your-soul way moms have. I hadn't told her about Ches. I didn't now. I gave her what I imagined was a lofty, CEO-type smile. "A waiter serving fried chicken versus a performer at the world-famous Keynote? Mom. Mom. Mom."

"Yes, Nate. I'm aware of our biological connection." She reached across, picked up the napkin beside my plate, and handed it to me. "If you're going to move in such august circles, you'd better remember your table manners."

I spread the napkin in my lap. Napkins were useful. You could hide food you didn't want to eat in them and later empty them out in the garbage. "Not just in August, Mom. Mike's thinking long-term."

She managed a faint smile at my joke. "I'm not sure Mike Dante is a nice person. He renovicts people. Forces them out of their homes so he can build luxury properties that few of us in this city can afford."

Nice. That was such a mom word. I wanted to say that successful people like Mike needed to have more going on than *nice*. He had to make big-dollar decisions. Had to stay ahead of the other guy. Operate in the key of surprise, like he said.

I was about to explain this. Then I thought of Mom, working in an office, assistant to the boss. Making appointments, typing, answering the phone. A quiet, unexciting job. She wouldn't, couldn't, understand about someone like Mike.

Instead I said, "Mike gave me the amount of money Fake Beethoven stole. That was nice of him."

"It was," she said, surprised. "Maybe he isn't so bad."

"Mike is going to be mega-good for us," I assured her. Spearing another piece of broccoli, I waved it dismissively at our surroundings. "Once my career takes off, I'll buy us our own place. No more cackling landladies, no more worrying about increases in rent or being renovicted."

That got a wistful smile out of Mom. I'd seen her fretting over news stories about developers getting the go-ahead to build condos in our 'hood near the Broadway SkyTrain station. Houses like Mrs. Snythe's were tumbling like pins in a bowling strike. I understood Mom's doubts. I got that she couldn't trust good news. Even true, real news, like the opportunity Mike was giving me. Mom was too used to the challenge of supporting us. To things being tough.

And, as it turned out, to my broccoli-disposal strategy. "You take that broccoli you're hiding in your napkin, put it back on your plate and eat it, Mr. Star Pianist."

But star pianists don't shine without

practice. To practise for my Keynote gig, I dropped everything else. Mom had to force water on me: "You'll dehydrate!" She also threatened to empty plates over my head if I didn't eat the food she'd put on them. I didn't think she'd really do it, but with nutrition you never knew what lengths moms will go to. I paused in practising to shove the food back without tasting it.

Sleep? That I saw no need for. Mom and I argued and finally settled on a compromise. Midnight was my piano curfew. And I couldn't start playing before 8 a.m.

This worked well. Until 10:00 p.m. one night. My new—well, new to me—Bose headphones blocked out landlady cackles and neighbour reality-show screams. But not my sense of feel. As I jumped in time with my playing, I felt seismic-power thumps pounding back at me from under the floor. I decided the old house's boiler was acting up and adapted my playing and jumping to the fast-paced thumps: *Bah-bah-bah-BOOM!* Cool.

The thumps ended. Moments later the

light in our front hall switched on. Mom was trudging out of bed to answer the door. Curious, I removed my headphones.

Our landlady glared at us. She was brandishing a broom and raging at Mom.

"I bashed at my ceiling over and over with the end of my broom!" The landlady was so angry she was almost crying. "I thought Nathan would take the hint. But he just kept jumping more fiercely. So inconsiderate."

Mom removed the earplugs she wore for sleeping. "I'm very sorry. I did leave you a note about Nate's practising, about his big opportunity. I included some earplugs and hoped that you would understand. You've always been so kind to us," Mom added.

The landlady paused. She sucked oxygen in and out of her long, thin nose, thinking. Finally she removed a package of earplugs from her apron pocket. "Hmph! I found these in my mailbox but haven't read your note yet. I pay bills first, look at other things after. I'm the prompt-paying type, as you may know."

We did know. Mrs. Snythe told us often.

Mom smiled, which seemed to thaw the landlady a bit. Shrugging, Snythe tossed the earplugs package at our table. Bad aim. They missed and hit the floor.

Snythe sniffed, as if the earplugs had done this to annoy her. "I don't like earplugs and I won't wear them. This noise is utterly unacceptable."

"Of course, Mrs. Snythe," Mom soothed. "Nate will only jump around in the daytime."

"But Mom, I have to—"

"Only in the daytime," Mom repeated to Mrs. Snythe, with one of her warning, you-want-us-to-lose-this-place? frowns at me.

With nonstop practice I would be sort of ready to play in the Keynote courtyard. *Sort of* being my best shot. Practice for me included jumping. Now, like a fallboard, our landlady had closed down my chance at that.

With intense effort I squelched an agonized, my-life-is-over-type yell.

Chapter Four

I held that yell for hours but it burst out the next day. Trish Laharne, Mike Dante's executive assistant, presented me with a contract for my summer gig in the court-yard. Not just for the summer, I saw, reading closer. The whole year, weekends when school was on, with an option to renew. Over those words Mike had scrawled and initialled, *You bet I'll renew, Rocker Crocker!*

That's when I let loose my agonized yell. Ms. Laharne asked what was wrong. I told her about Mrs. Snythe.

Laharne strode to Mike's door and walked right in—even though he had someone with him. Said, "Nate has a problem. Some old witch won't let him practise piano the way he needs to."

And that did it. In the world of Dante, I was discovering, your wish became Mike's command. Ten minutes later the burly security guard was letting me into the Andante restaurant to practise all I wanted on the gleaming black grand. Laharne gave me a keycard so I could swipe my way in any time of day or night. And Dante Enterprises would pay for cab rides home in the dark.

"Anything you need, you ask," the guard said, before leaving me to play—well, for the first while, gawk—at the grand. "My name's Sladen, by the way."

He couldn't quite manage a smile. That was okay. Smiles weren't in his nature. Being here, having my practice problem solved, was enough for me.

After that I spent every evening at the Andante. Played for hours. Jumped, shouted, sang at the top of my lungs. I asked if I could keep practising at night after I started work. Sure, Mike said. The restaurant wouldn't open for at least another month. Until then, the place was mine.

Ms. Laharne texted me to check the fridge when I came in. Sandwiches, pickles, brownies, milk cartons, pop cans waited for me. Beside the fridge, bags of chips and pretzels. One day two free-dinner coupons for the Andante were stuck on the fridge door, along with a note: *We're sending these to the thief's victims. The least we can do. Bring your mom! — Mike*.

Life was good. I practised and snacked, practised and snacked. Beethoven was often in the room, scowling when I couldn't get notes right and wanted to give up. Nodding, though never smiling, when I finally did get the notes. Before, Beethoven — well, my ghostly vision of him — had materialized occasionally. Now this ghostly vision showed up every day while I got ready for my debut. My own personal trainer/nagger.

The night before my first day performing, Beethoven strolled in. I was rocking out *The Fifth,* so I didn't notice right away that this

Beethoven wasn't my somewhat-friendly ghost. This vision was flesh and blood. With a discordant jumble of notes I stopped. A ghastly, not ghostly, possibility occurred to me: Was this the fourth Beethoven? *Was this the thief?*

We stared at each other. Then he peeled off his mask. "You look like you're seeing a ghost," Bo Dante said.

I let out a relieved breath. "It does happen."

Bo laughed. He held out a rectangular black velvet box. On the lid a rhinestone quarter note glistened. "For you. From Dad. Was going to bring it himself. But he's stuck in a meeting," he finished with a yawn.

I noticed how he spoke in short, clipped sentences. Conserving his energy, I decided. I remembered Bo collapsing on the sofa in his dad's office. I'd thought he was lazy. Now I saw it was more than that. The guy was nonstop sleepy, possibly a medical condition.

He flopped down on a chair and put his feet up on a table. "Go ahead, bud.

Open it." Right. Mike's gift. I lifted the lid. A sleek black pen studded with another rhinestone quarter note gleamed up at me. Tucked beside the pen was Mike Dante's business card with a scrawled message: *Because I like employees who shine to have shining rewards—M.D.*

"Wow," I breathed. I lifted the pen. What a beaut. It was enough to make me want to take up handwriting.

Bo's reply was a loud snore. A kid my age, asleep at 7:00 p.m.? Yeah, something was wrong there.

I carefully put the glittery pen back in its box. Set the box on top of the piano. Poised my fingers over the keys to start playing again.

And didn't. The way I played wasn't exactly lullaby mode. As Mrs. Snythe had once sniped, my music was enough to rattle skeletons out of their graves.

Snipey Snythe, complaining about my music. Tossing earplugs at our table—and missing. Later I'd picked them up and tucked them into the pockets of my shorts

That gave me an idea.

I fished in my pockets. As long as these were the same shorts I'd been wearing the other night, the plugs should be there. And I rarely switched outfits day to day. Much more efficient, I found, to grab yesterday's duds in their easy-to-find heap on the floor.

Sure enough, my fingers closed on the plugs. *Et voilà*, as my French teacher would say. Or, in this case, *Ear voilà.*

Stepping over to Sleeping Bo-ty, I fit the plugs in his ears. He didn't even stir. I returned to the grand and practised. For a while I kept checking on Bo. Then I forgot he was there. It was only me and the music. I jumped and jived *The Fifth* until the crystals in the Andante's chandelier tinkled. Until sweat ran down into my eyes. Through blurred eyes I saw Ludwig van Beethoven smiling. The real Ludwig—that is, the real ghost.

"Whoa," I exclaimed. Beethoven, smiling. A first.

"Whoa," said Bo Dante. He sat up, jabbed at his smart watch. "Weird. I felt the

43

alarm vibrate but didn't hear it. And I always set the volume at max so I won't miss—" He winced. "Hey, what's with these?" He peeled the plugs from his ears.

"So I wouldn't disturb you," I explained. I crashed out *bah-bah-bah-BOOM* by way of explanation.

"Right. Rocker Crocker." Bo smiled, a big smile like his dad's. "Thanks for that." He stood up, stretched. Touched his hands to his toes several times, jogged on the spot, fell to the floor and did push-ups. Then ran around the room, lifting his knees high.

I watched in disbelief. Not only was Sleeping Bo-ty totally juiced, he was speaking in full sentences. "I thought you were into napping."

He laughed, "I go sailing, ten p.m. to midnight. Four nights of the week I take lessons. The other three I go out with buddies. And Dad insists I work in the daytime."

I nodded. I'd had Bo wrong. He wasn't lazy. He wasn't suffering from some all-sleep-all-the-time medical condition. He was a night sailor.

"You sail, Rocker?"

I remembered Ches and me, kids on the beach at Trout Lake. We brought blocks of wood with folded paper glued to the blocks so the rest of the paper stood up straight like sails. Boats with sails, to nine-year-old eyes. And the lake was the big wide ocean.

"Yeah. No. Not really," I said, missing Ches.

"Try night sailing sometime," Bo urged. "There's nothing like it. The dark air hurling at you. The moon ducking in and out of clouds. The waves you feel more than see." He jogged around the room one more time, stopped and then ran on the spot. "I mean, you can't play piano all the time."

Now it was Mrs. Snythe I was seeing. Mrs. Snythe, years ago, smirking as she cackled, *It's not like Nate's interest in piano is going to last, not the way he plays.*

"Someone did once tell me I couldn't."

Bo picked up his Beethoven mask, twirled it at me in a goodbye gesture. "You're okay, Rocker Crocker. I'll see you around. And don't forget: night sailing."

"I will. I mean, I won't. Forget, that is. Thanks." I watched Bo sprint out of the restaurant. Me on a sailboat. Right. When Mom and I camped at Lightning Lake in Manning Park, I brought bathing trunks. That was the extent of my water-sports gear. Still, Bo was being friendly, and I appreciated that. He was like his dad: even with all those Dante dollars, not a snob.

But I wasn't the sailboat type. *The dark air hurling at you.* I had a feeling it would be me hurling into the dark air.

I wished Ches were around. He'd hoot at that. He hooted loudly at all my feeble jokes. I liked Ches's hoot-laugh.

With a force of will I pushed Ches from my mind. Time to practise. *Mr. Star Pianist*, Mom had called me. I felt good about that. I felt that way right up to my first morning on the job. When I stood in the Keynote lobby and looked out to the courtyard. To the piano waiting for me, a silver one with black quarter notes painted on the sides.

And stage fright froze me.

Chapter Five

This couldn't be happening. Not my first day on the job, my first set. I had to play. I had to wow Mike Dante and show him he was right to believe in me.

I straightened my shoulders in my red *Dante Enterprises* T-shirt. I pinned on my *Nate Crocker, Dante Enterprises* name badge. Grasped the red Dante Enterprises cap Mike had said I should put upside down on the piano for tips. With my employer's name all over me, I couldn't screw up.

Mike and his assistant were over by the elevator. Laharne was reading off her phone. "Martha Shulman is stuck at the Hong Kong airport. Won't be able to make tomorrow's meeting." She dropped the phone into her purse. "No worries, boss.

Martha will send her notes to me. I'll fill in for her. I'll take care of it. Of course I'll have to visit my stylist first. Want to look my best for our investors!" Whinnying, she patted her straw-blonde hair.

I smoothed down my own unruly hair. Any excuse to delay going out there. *Maybe I should pop home for a second shower*, I thought.

"No, the hair is good," Mike called, beaming. "Sticking out all over like that is perfect. The Beethoven look, like you have a finger plugged in a socket. All the better to make people notice you. Now go get 'em, champ."

"Yessir," I said. Or rather, squeaked. I tried to keep Mom's words in mind: *Stage fright is your friend. It means you care about your performance*. *It means you'll give it your all out there.*

I didn't trust myself not to squeak again, so I just nodded to Mike. I walked out to the piano.

I gently raised the fallboard. A few people noticed me. The rest kept gawking upward.

I sat down, started tinkling out "Ode to Joy." At home I played it my usual way, fast, loud and staccato. Putting the *joy* in the *ode*, if you will.

Now, nervous about making a mistake, I played the notes slowly, quietly. I glanced around. Most people were still looking up. That was good. If nobody paid attention to me, nobody would hear my mistakes. Play so no one can hear: the stress-free approach to performing.

Beethoven stomped up to me, hair blowing wildly. My Beethoven, not one of the costumed ones. He leaned over the piano and scowled.

I gave him a mind-your-own-business scowl back. Why should he care about some kid playing easy versions of his tunes?

But he out-scowled me. For a figment of my imagination he was competitive.

My fingers slid off the piano. I stared at the keys. I'd practised and practised, barely sleeping or eating. *I can't do this*, I mentally told Ludwig. *Nerves have got to me*.

Beethoven faded away without saying

anything. I knew he had never been afraid. It was just the opposite. A writer of his time described Beethoven's personality as "utterly untamed."

I grew angry. If nerves were attacking, I would attack back. That's what Beethoven would do.

I got up, shoving the bench backward so hard it fell on its side. I didn't care. No more scaredy-cat playing.

I bashed the ode out, THUMP-pah, THUMP-pah. I jumped side to side. I started on another tune. I knew performers were supposed to stop between songs, smile, thank people for being there. But that was polite. I wasn't in the mood for polite.

Next I played one of Mom's favourites, the jazzy standard "Sweet Georgia Brown." I heard the lyrics in my head bouncing along with me, so I belted them out:

"Two left feet, oh, so neat, has Sweet Georgia Brown!"

"Georgia" has been the theme song of the Harlem Globetrotters since 1952. I thought of the Globetrotters shooting hoop after hoop with that tune in their heads. It made me smile. I wasn't angry anymore.

Instead of anger, energy now burned through me. Firing up my fingertips, sizzling the keys. "Georgia claimed her, Georgia named her!" I shouted. I bashed the notes out louder, jumped around even more.

Mom said my energy was relate to my impatience. My energy was productive and meant I'd do creative things in a big way.

She said impatience was unproductive. *So. Don't. Be. Impatient*.

I wasn't feeling impatient now. For a finale I ran the ball of my fist all the way down the keys. I stepped back, grinned. There'd been mistakes, but I'd stopped being scared and played like me. I'd sent the notes rocking up through the stratosphere.

Then I forgot about the stratosphere. Because here on earth the crowd was cheering, clapping, whistling. They pushed forward, jostling each other, to put money on top of the piano.

A woman with long, dark-red hair carried her little boy over. With a pudgy hand the kid slapped down a fiver. Then he bashed his fingers on invisible keys and howled, "Two left feet, can't wait to eat sweet Georgia brownies!"

I laughed. "No doubt about it, Junior. One day you'll have your own musical cooking show."

The woman's eyes sparkled. She sure was pretty. She said, "You've done the impossible. You've inspired my son. His dad keeps trying to teach him music, but Randall is stubborn. Until now he's refused even to look at a piano."

I thought about adults who urged me to do things. Like our piano-teacher landlady who offered to give me lessons at a cheap rate. *If you're serious about music, you should be serious about lessons.* And every weekend I saw the miserable faces of Mrs. Snythe's students. Serious about lessons. Yeah, deathly serious.

Randall was still bashing invisible keys and shouting his version of the "Georgia Brown" lyrics. In a low voice I told his mom, "Maybe Randall's dad should lay off."

Her eyes widened. *Uh-oh, #tooblunt*, I thought. But she was smiling. "That's what I keep saying. But Randall's dad is the intense type. He won't listen."

I thought back to how I got into piano: listening to my mom play, watching her fingers on the keys. Seeing how she smiled when she escaped into the music. Instead of telling me to play piano, she'd shown me I might like it.

I tried to explain this. The woman nodded. She glanced at my nametag. "Nice to meet you, Nate. I'm Mallory Sherman." She held out her hand.

I clasped it. I thought what a great tradition the handshake was. It gave you a good, close-up look at the person you were meeting. At their smile that seemed to stretch forever.

Mallory said, "Ummm…"

Long moments were ticking by and I was still holding her hand. I let go. "Sorry, ma'am. Er, Mallory. I should get on with…" Embarrassed, I tried to remember what I was supposed to be doing. "Right. Playing."

I lowered my fingers to the keys. Except my fingers never got there.

A sign sliced down in front of my face, blocking my view. "Mike Dante is a liar, liar, pants on fire!" shouted a voice in my ear.

It was a girl. *The* girl. Zandi Singh, the thief's second victim. Her dark eyes blazed. Behind her, several others took up the shout, "Mike Dante, liar, liar, pants on fire!"

I grabbed the sign from Zandi. *This is what a home looks like*, read the top line. Underneath, a drawing of a low-rise, yellow-painted clapboard apartment building surrounded by trees. A nice drawing, preferable to the X-through-Mike's-face signs. The building reminded me of Mrs. Snythe's old, rambling house—friendly, comfortable.

With my free hand I bashed out bah-bah-bah-*boom*. Mike had given me a portable speaker but I didn't need it. I was loud enough to drown out the shouters.

"Mike finds homes for people who have

to move because of his developments," I said. "The city gave him an award for that."

She shook her head, her short, dark curls bouncing angrily. "You can't just move people out of the way and dump them somewhere else. We're not landfill."

"Mike moved you into a garbage dump? That's where you're living?"

"Well, no, but—"

"I'm betting he found a home for you. A new beginning."

"You don't get it, piano player. Up to six months ago, we lived in an apartment off Main Street, near Queen Elizabeth Park. We loved it. It was our home. I'd lived there all my life. We had friends close by, school down the street. Then we got the land-lord's notice. We got renovicted, tossed out before our lease was up. That's what I mean: like landfill, not tenants."

Renovictions. That's what Mom always worried about.

I was aware of the crowd muttering and starting to turn away. They expected entertainment.

So, I went for funny. "Wait. *Ten*ants? Not twenty or thirty ants?"

This didn't get any yuks from Zandi and her buddies. Not my best material, I'll admit. But others laughed. Someone called out, "Let the kid play!"

Zandi flinched and limped back a few steps. I remembered the thief barreling into her, knocking her over. "Hey, sorry about your ankle."

"Don't change the subject. Mike Dante lied. He promised—"

"Let the kid play!" people shouted.

Then Randall took matters into his own hands. Or rather, his own feet.

I still had the sign. I was holding it upside down, resting the part with the drawing on the ground.

Randall kicked—first with one foot, then the other—clean through the sign.

Chapter Six

Before he could launch another kick, I gave the sign back to Zandi.

Mallory told her, "My son is very sorry."

Zandi eyed Randall doubtfully. There wasn't a whole lot of sorry in his expression.

The Keynote's burly security guard stomped up. "You're disrupting the public peace," Sladen bellowed.

Zandi waved her sign. "No! People need to hear me out."

Actually, people were laughing. I looked more closely at the sign. In one of his kicks, Randall's shoe had come off. It was wedged right under the words *This is what a home looks like.*

The guard wrenched the sign away from Zandi. He crunched it in half, crumpling the placard and shattering the wood post. Tossing the pieces on the ground, he ordered Zandi and her buddies to leave me alone. "Or else!" He swaggered off.

Everyone stood in shocked silence. The guy was like King Kong.

The silence began to ring in my ears. Mike was paying me to play.

I jumped back to the keyboard, bashed out a second round of the *Fifth.* The crowd smiled, swayed in time with the music. Randall leaped side to side like I was doing. He waved his arms wildly, like a windmill in a storm.

I was stoked. I crushed. I *killed*.

I swept the ball of my fist down the keys, then up again. I closed my eyes and let the applause and the sun wash over me. Against my eyelids Beethoven appeared. He was still scowling but he nodded as if pleased.

I knew the story behind the *Fifth*'s famous opening. Beethoven wrote the bah-bah-bah-*boom* to represent fate knocking on his door. This moment was fate knocking on mine. Telling me that performing was what I was meant to do.

I opened my eyes to see my boss smiling at me. "I couldn't be prouder of you," Mike said. "Enthusiastic, friendly, welcoming. Just the image I want for Dante Enterprises."

He raised his voice and spoke to the crowd. "Is this kid hot or what?" He paused for whoops and cheers. "I'd say we have a star in the making. When you buy concert tickets for Nate Crocker in New York or Vegas, remember you first saw him here at the Keynote."

This was some moment. Mike's praise, the crowd roaring. I wanted to bronze the moment, keep it forever.

Not everyone felt the same. In the happy crowd one glum person stuck out like a sore—well, a sore ankle. Zandi sat hunched on a bench over by the news vendor.

Poor kid. That was a wallop she'd taken from the rampaging thief. Talk about King Kong. The guy had smashed her to the ground.

Stop. Rewind. *Talk about King Kong*.

A crazy thought hit me: *Could Sladen be the fourth Beethoven?* The guard had the thief's grab-and-go strength. And working at the Keynote, he would know where the costumes were kept.

After randomly targeting his victims, the thief had run into the Keynote. He'd escaped through the restaurant—so I'd thought. But if the guard was the thief, he could have changed back into his Keynote uniform. It had been several minutes before he'd nabbed me for trespassing.

No, I thought. Couldn't be. Mike Dante was big-time smart. He would make careful hires. No criminals. The thief couldn't be a Dante employee. Impossible.

On my break I strolled over to Zandi. Alone on the bench, she was calling out to pass-ersby, trying to get signatures for a petition to city council to stop renovictions.

I sat down beside her. The petition didn't have a lot of names.

"What happened to your buddies?" I asked.

Zandi shrugged. "Nobody's paying attention to us. They went to a park down the street where it's"— she slid me a sideways look—"quieter."

I took the clipboard with the petition on it. A pen rested along the top. I read over the petition. It didn't mention Mike Dante, just objected to the continuing, large-scale tossing out of low- or average-income tenants from old buildings. Then tossing up swanky buildings for high-income earners.

I couldn't argue with that. Low- or average-income: in other words, regular people like Mom and me. And it could happen to Mom and me. Worse, if Mrs. Snythe did sell, it might not be to a developer like Mike Dante, who found new homes for renovicted tenants.

I added my name to the list of signatures.

"Thanks," Zandi said.

I got another sideways look, this one almost friendly. "You're not worried Mike Dante will find out you signed this?"

The idea was so ridiculous I laughed. "Mike Dante has never told me what to sign or not sign. He doesn't care. He wants me to play. And I will, because this is my big chance. I'll play, play, play and get better and better. I know I will. Stay with what you like and eventually you'll get rewarded."

Whoa. I clamped my motormouth shut. What prompted me to share all that? Maybe it was the wary expression Zandi always had with me. Most people liked me right away, joked around with me. Like they liked Mike Dante. I guess I wanted Zandi to feel like that, too. Or at least to see I was human.

Briefly something like understanding glinted in her dark eyes. Very briefly. She shut it down and gave me a sardonic grin. "Wow. You should make motivational videos."

"So much sarcasm in one so young. It's sad." I checked my phone. My fifteen-minute break was ticking down. "I'm here to talk crime, not music. I wondered if you noticed anything about the thief. Other than the Beethoven costume, I mean."

She shook her head. "I didn't see him until he smashed into me. I was heading to an appointment with Mr. Dante. That's what I was thinking about."

"An appointment with Mike?"

"Ohhh, first-name basis. Yeah, with *Mike*. I had a meeting to talk to him about losing our home. Instead I met up with the thief"

"So make another appointment. Mike will hear you out. He's a good listener."

She frowned. "Please. With a selfish, profit-first guy like that, it's pointless."

I frowned back. Our moment of almost-friendliness was over. I wondered why she wouldn't give Mike a chance. Instead she showed up here day after day, waving signs and shouting. Maybe she just liked being angry.

I stood. "Forget it. Sorry to bother you."

She sighed. "Okay, wait. Why are you asking about the thief? Did *you* notice something?"

"Yeah. A nervous tic. He's into knuckle cracking." I made the popping sounds with my lips.

"Stop!" she exclaimed.

"C'mon, I've been practising." Sheesh. Nobody appreciated sound effects.

But it wasn't me Zandi was speaking to. It was a dad and two kids. She held out the petition, explained about Mike Dante forcing people from their homes.

The dad smiled at her—and asked me when I'd be playing again.

"Soon," I promised. Annoying as I found Zandi, I felt bad for her. Injured *and* ignored. On impulse I pulled a package of green licorice from my back pocket. "Everyone's supposed to include greens in their diet, so here. One of my favourites, just for you."

She didn't look overly thrilled. Then I remembered Constable Barker's victims' list. "Oh, right," I said. "You're into carrots."

She looked startled. "How did you know that?"

"Psychic. I see all, know all." I checked my phone. Showtime.

The scent of mango distracted me. Mango wasn't what my nostrils were used to around here. The air tended to be a mix of sea smells and coffee. I turned. It was Mallory Sherman. The scent was coming off her hair. *Must be her shampoo*, I thought.

"Hey," I said. "You smell—"

A blast of horns from down by the water interrupted me. *O Ca-na-da!* Every day at noon the famous Heritage Horns at Canada Place blasted out the start of our national anthem.

I said awkwardly, "Uh…about you smelling. I didn't mean that the way it sounded."

Behind me, Zandi snorted.

Mallory laughed. "It's fine." Her face grew serious. "I wanted to talk to you about meeting up later today."

I was stunned. She couldn't mean what I thought. That she wanted to meet me—unsuave me—alone.

Discordant notes crashed through my brain. This wasn't right. I needed to point this out. By now, however, I had lost all language skills. All I got out was, "Bbflfigglmtch."

She studied me, concerned. "Are you all right, Nate?"

"Sure. I'm just…uh…" I tugged at the

neck of my T-shirt. I was having trouble breathing.

I coughed. "If you're into burgers, the concession at Canadian Tire is fairly decent. Packets of ketchup, mustard and relish are all free. As are salt and pepper." And there would be people around, I added mentally. None of this meet-alone stuff.

Then I noticed Mallory's expression. Total bewilderment.

Chapter Seven

Mallory said, "I don't need to shop at Canadian Tire, Nate. I want to speak to you about Randall. You got through to him with your enthusiasm for music. Randall doesn't always take to people. Much of the time he's off in his own world. That's the way it is with kids on the spectrum."

Relief swept through me. Of course she hadn't meant an *alone* alone meeting. "Listen," I said. "I don't know about spectrums, but I see Ludwig van Beethoven several times a day. We communicate. Well, he communicates with me. Usually via scowls." I stopped, hoping she wouldn't find my Ludwig sightings too weird. "What I'm saying is, so what if Randall is different? I totally get different."

Mallory relaxed into a big smile. "That's wonderful because I was wondering: Could I hire you to entertain the kids at Randall's birthday party later today?"

My relief gave way to sheer horror. I could take Randall in small doses. But a houseful of Randalls? This was *not* what I had in mind for a music career. Or for my mental health. "Are you kidding? No way!"

Mallory drew back. Her eyes widened.

Oh no, you don't, I thought. *You're not getting to me with that hurt look. Not this boy.*

I began, "It's just that I don't like—" *Say it, Crocker. Tell her you don't like small fry.* Instead I heard myself replying weakly, "What I meant was, no way I'd refuse. A birthday party with Randall. And his little friends, too. Wow."

Mallory beamed. "That's great! What time do you finish here?"

"Two o'clock," I mumbled.

"We'll have you in just before hot dogs and chocolate cake." Mallory told me her address, then hurried off.

I tapped the address into my phone contacts. Tapped it slowly, not unlike the beat of Chopin's "Funeral March."

From the bench Zandi gave me a mocking smile. "You handled *that* well, piano player."

I knew she was reading me like a book. A pathetic book titled *Awww, Nate Has a Crush*.

I thought of Ludwig van Beethoven. He, too, had a crush on a married woman. He turned his feelings into something creative: the *Seventh Symphony*.

My crush would also result in music. Not quite the same, though. At Randall's birthday party I'd be playing *Old MacDonald Had a Farm*.

My second break rolled around. I needed it. Not because I was tired. Because I was soaking in sweat. By now the sun was blazing straight down. As I pounded out another round of "Sweet Georgia Brown," drops from my forehead hit the keys.

I dragged out the last few notes, shouting the lyrics along with them: "Sweet! Georgia! Browwwwwn!" The crowd cheered and whistled. They piled coins and bills into my upturned cap until it overflowed. I wiped sweat off my forehead with the back of my arm — what I really needed was a mop — and grinned around at everyone.

Two Beethovens strolled by. "Bo?" I said uncertainly.

Through their scowling masks the two Beethovens laughed. One said, "Nope. We're his buddies, Connor and Devon. Bo's snoozing in his old man's office."

Night-sailor Bo. Of course he'd be snoozing. I studied the second and third Beethovens. They were identical: the same messy wig, scowling mask, frilly white shirt and black pants. Just like Bo.

And just like the fourth Beethoven. The thief.

I thought again of the security guard. If he was the thief, he'd have needed shirt and pants a size bigger. I tried to recall if the fourth Beethoven had been burly. I couldn't.

It had happened too fast. "Where did you guys get your costumes?" I asked.

Beethovens Two and Three glanced at each other and chuckled. They rapped their foreheads like they were knocking on a door.

And I thought *my* jokes were feeble.

Two and Three turned away to hand out brochures. I gave up on the idea of learning anything from them.

I headed into the lobby. I found a drinking fountain, turned it on and dunked my head under. The security guard was at the reception desk. I thought he might object. But he didn't. I shut my eyes and savored the refreshing mini-shower.

And then I heard it. *Pop! Pop! Pop!*

The sound of knuckles cracking.

I stood up, wiped water from my eyes. If that was the security guard, I'd been right. He was the thief.

But the *pop, pop, pop!* wasn't knuckles.

The guard was slamming a hammer down on the reception desk. The raised counter prevented me from seeing what he was demolishing—until he crammed a handful of green nuts into his mouth. He was using the hammer to open pistachios. Talk about nuts.

Me, I needed solid nutrition. I found a lunch joint, sat by a window and scarfed down a burger and fries.

Being talented at multi-tasking, I also studied an easy-sheet-music version of "Moonlight Sonata." As usual, Ludwig had broken the rules in writing it. Up to then, sonata movements had gone fast, slow, fast. He'd written "Moonlight Sonata" slow, medium, fast. Which meant I couldn't rock out the first two movements.

Zandi walked by the window, tapping the keypad of a sparkly pink cellphone.

Stuffing the sheet music into my back-pack, I grabbed my burger and jogged outside to catch up with her. "The cops found your phone?"

"Oh, it's you, lover boy." She said with

a scornful glance at my burger, which was leaking mustard.

"So I like mustard," I said. "What's your preferred condiment—superiority?"

"Mildly amusing, as always, Crocker." Zandi held the phone up. The pink wasn't just sparkles. It was sparkly chips that stuck out all over like teeth. In the noon sun they scalded my eyes. "My replacement phone. About all that was in my budget."

I recalled Constable Barker's victims' list. "Now you're just missing a bag of carrots and a *Give Us Back Our Homes!* file."

"The file I can't replace. Stupidly, I didn't make a copy."

"What was in it?"

She shot me one of her scornful looks. "You wouldn't understand."

And *you*, I thought, *have a chip on your shoulder a thousand times the size of those pink ones*. No, I didn't understand. Still, shoulder chip or not, Zandi looked so unhappy I tried to joke her out of it. "The real loser was the woman who lost a pair of ruby earrings. Now *those* were carats."

This got me a faint smile. Then Zandi went off to find shade. Hard to use a phone when it's sun-blinding you.

I went back to the piano. *Carrots and carats*, I thought. It no longer seemed funny. Something about *carrots and carats* bothered me.

But I didn't have time to think about it. I had Beethoven's *Fifth* to rock out. After work I wouldn't have time, either. I had to go entertain a bunch of kiddies.

I wondered if Ludwig ever got stuck performing for the recently-out-of-diapers set.

I had some time before I went to the Shermans', so I used it to SkyTrain home to East Van. I had a package I needed to drop off at Ches's. A gift for him, to make up for quitting Charlie's Chicken after he'd recommended me. To try to make up for it, anyway.

Nobody answered when I buzzed. I then buzzed the manager, asked her to deliver the gift to Ches. She looked at it doubtfully. What, she had a problem with presents wrapped in a Safeway-specials-of-the-week flyer? But she took it.

I caught a 99 Express bus to the west side. I got off at the Shermans' street. They lived near the beach, in a townhouse behind a huge wall of purple rhododendrons.

Thanks to the thick rhodos, I almost missed seeing a woman wheeling out an empty stroller at Indy 500 speed. Having just dumped off little Becky or Bobby, she was no doubt in a rush to enjoy her free time. I jumped away from the oncoming stroller with nanoseconds to spare.

I knocked on the Shermans' door. Randall opened it. He had sunglasses on.

"Wearing shades indoors, huh?" I said.

"Nobody can make me not wear them."

A little girl appeared beside him. "Hey, you didn't notice my new dress!" she accused—and hurled a beach ball at Randall's head.

He ducked. The ball struck a vase, knocking it over and shattering it. Yeah, this was going to be a great afternoon.

"Nate!" Mallory waded through the kids to greet me.

The little girl was staring at the broken pieces of vase. She began to cry. In my back pocket I still had napkin-wrapped fries. Kind of squashed, but so what. I held them out. "Have some potatoes. They're the type that's bad for you."

Her eyes formed startled Os. But she stopped crying and shoved the fries into her mouth.

"Behaviour modification," I explained to Mallory.

Randall's mom giggled. She took me by the arm and guided me through the living room to a grand piano. Ni-i-ice.

Mallory said, "I thought we'd play musical chairs. Then, sit and eat with the kids. Does that sound okay?"

I didn't reply. I'd noticed a framed photo on top of the grand. The sun caught on the glass, but I made out a man in the photo. He looked fierce and had a fist raised, like he was about to punch through the glass.

"That's my husband Gerald," said Mallory.

I remembered Mallory describing him as the intense type. Intense was putting it mildly. I hoped I never crossed paths with Gerald. If he suspected I liked Mallory, his idea of behaviour modification might involve teeth removal.

Chapter Eight

Randall joined us. He stared up. In his sunglasses our reflections stared up, too.

"Sweetie, how can you see with those on?" his mom exclaimed.

"Nobody can make me take them off."

Mallory kept her voice bright. "Nate is going to play for you and your guests. Won't that be fun? Maybe it will make you want to try piano yourself."

"Nobody can—"

"We get it, we get it," I assured Randall. "You'd rather step off the top of the Keynote without a parachute."

Randall's jaw dropped. I bent to look inside. "Hello? Anyone in there?"

While Mallory herded the kids, I brought chairs in from the dining room. I arranged them in two back-to-back rows. Musical chairs. What a thing to use a grand piano for.

I sat down at the piano. I turned the hostile husband photo away from me and started playing "Old MacDonald." That grew depressing fast. I switched to "Sweet Georgia Brown," with frequent stops for kids to plunk into seats. I hoped the Harlem Globetrotters never heard about this.

Mallory kept taking chairs away from one side, then another. Now only Randall and the girl who had wailed were left, with one chair in the middle. I stopped playing. The two of them crammed on the last chair. The girl instantly started wailing. Randall said nobody could make him get up. Mallory called it a tie.

I turned my back to the kiddies and played more "Georgia Brown." I played it slow and quiet, to let Mallory speak to the kids and be heard.

I didn't often play quiet. It let me think. I was remembering musical chairs when I was a kid. The giggles and screams, the crashing of bodies scrambling for chairs.

Now, from my lofty perspective, the way to win was obvious. While the kids moved around to the music, an adult took a chair from either side. The last remaining chair would be one of the two back-to-back in dead centre. The other chairs were just a distraction.

If I'd known as a tot to keep my eye on the centre, I would have killed at musical chairs. I rippled the piano keys up and down and laughed at the thought.

The other chairs were just a distraction. I played slow again, thinking. I was picturing a different game. Not musical chairs. Musical robberies.

There was a rash of purse and wallet grabs lately The fourth Beethoven seemed to fit in with that, to be a random thief. But suppose he wasn't random? He'd targeted me, Zandi and the woman—what was her name? Oh yeah. Susan Volker. With Susan he'd scored rubies. What if he'd known she was taking the earrings in for repair?

My brain revved up. I sped up the tempo of the music in time with it. Say the thief wanted to grab Susan's purse. To make it look random, he robbed two other people he didn't know: me and Zandi.

That's why *carats* versus *carrots* had stuck in my brain. A thief would aim for carats, not carrots.

The thief had fooled the cops into investigating three robberies. If they focused on just the theft of rubies, they might narrow down the suspects.

"Sweet Georgia Brown!" I shouted, now up and jumping. On the table, plates and glasses rattled. And whoa—outside the window the rhododendrons rustled.

The kids caught my excitement. They jumped with me and clapped their hands.

I grinned at them. They were cute.

Wait. There were cute kids?

I played more tunes, kept the kids rocking. I couldn't wait to talk with Constable Barker. If I was right, the fourth Beethoven was someone Susan Volker knew.

I tucked back two hot dogs. Between the ketchup and relish I more than got my vegetable requirements for the evening.

I went back to the piano. On my phone I brought up easy sheet music to "Moonlight Sonata." Propping my phone on the rack, I started studying the sonata. I'd just played quiet, so I figured I should be able to play the sonata. Loud was fun, but I was learning quiet could be cool.

Before my fingers touched the keys, my phone rang. I looked at the caller ID and grinned. "Ches!" I exclaimed into the phone.

Ches's voice blared out, "The building manager brought me your gift. A *pen*. What's the idea? Who uses *pens*?"

I didn't bother lowering the volume. No matter what the setting, Ches was a loud, eardrum-splitting kind of guy. I did what I always had to do: put the phone on speaker and push it a few feet away from me.

"It's a peace offering," I said. "An apology for walking out of Charlie's Chicken without notice. It's a nice pen, Ches."

A blast of scornful words, too fast and

loud to understand, greeted this. Apparently Ches thought pens were…"Useless!" he bellowed.

"I'm just trying to say sorry." I thought quickly. Ches was into cooking. "Hey, I know! Maybe you could use the pen for stirring. You know, soups, sauces, whatever."

I won't repeat the words Ches used in response. I ended the call. Mallory had taken the kidlets out front to wait for parents. In theory they were out of hearing range. But I didn't want to take any chances.

I started in on the easy version of "Moonlight Sonata." Thoughts of Ches, of the kids outside, of parents arriving, faded. When I was learning a song, it was all I thought about.

Even the easy-sheet-music sonata was a challenge. That was okay. The notes would come. I'd get them. I'd make them mine.

"See, Randall? This is how you get to be a piano player: by practising! You could practise on that nice little piano we got you."

Mallory and the kid were standing nearby. Everyone else had left.

Randall scowled. "Nobody can make me."

His mom just sighed. She looked disappointed.

I got up to go. I'd work on the sonata at home.

"Wait a sec, I'll get your money." Mallory hurried off.

I felt bad for her. *Randall, off in his own world,* she'd said. She had been so sure I was getting through to him.

But Randall was a stubborn kid. Though pride and stubbornness didn't mean he couldn't get into music. I thought about how I first had.

When I was bashing out my first notes with stubby kindergarten fingers, our landlady knocked at the door. Mrs. Snythe brandished a bill the postman had put in her mail slot by mistake. I heard her cackle to Mom, "This is yours, dear. Marked 'payment overdue,' I see. Tsk, tsk! Now I myself always pay on—my goodness, is that the *Fifth Symphony* little Nathan is bashing out? Beethoven is for serious students. Let Nate have fun with simple tunes.

It's not like his interest in piano is going to last, not the way he plays."

Something happened. My fingers tingled. They wanted back on the keys, bad. It was like Beethoven was talking to them, to me, through his music. Like he was saying, *You're the one playing my music, not Sour-Grapes Snythe.* I turned back, unclenched my fingers and continued bashing.

That's how Beethoven became my favourite. Sure, I liked playing other stuff. But with Beethoven it was as if he were standing nearby, encouraging me. Scowling, of course, never smiling. That's the way he was.

"Where's this piano your mom was talking about?" I asked.

Randall pointed a pudgy forefinger into the next room. I strode in. Randall followed. If I'd asked him to follow, he wouldn't have. But I was wise to Mr. Nobody-Can-Make-Me.

I sat down at his piano. "Can I play it?"

Randall shook his head. "It's mine. I'm not going to play it. Nobody else can, either."

I bent to Randall's eye level. "Nobody can make me *not* play it."

My knees wouldn't fit underneath the piano, so I had to jut them up against it. I started on "Sweet Georgia Brown." With my knees blocking my view of the keys, it wasn't my greatest performance. I didn't care. I bashed the notes out semi-correctly and howled the lyrics.

I finished one round. Randall poked a stubby finger in my shoulder. "I said you couldn't play my piano."

I swivelled to face him. "But I have to play it." Again I remembered Mrs. Snythe telling Mom I wouldn't keep playing. It was branded into my memory. It still burned.

"I'm like you. The can't-make-me type," I told Randall.

His mouth was a big, round whole note. I had him interested.

I tried to explain it the way Mom had to me. "Music, the really good music, is about just that: nobody-can-make-me. Composers are defiant. No matter how people try to talk them out of it, they create their own sound. When Beethoven was your age, he learned violin. But he refused to play the notes he was given. He made up his own. His dad got mad, said Beethoven was playing trash and would never amount to anything. Lucky for us, little Ludwig didn't listen. He kept doing his own thing."

Randall frowned. "Beethoven was playing trash? I thought he was playing the violin."

He hadn't understood. Of course he hadn't. He was a kidlet. A lecture on music appreciation was beyond him.

Mallory came back. She pressed bills into my hand. I gaped at them. This was more than your average babysitting fee. She laughed at my expression. Everybody found me funny. I might not get the girl but I always got the laughs.

She said, "Nate, you are the best party entertainer ever. The kids are raving about you to their parents. I'm betting more gigs will come your way if you want them."

Kiddie ent? I wanted to play clubs one day, not the *Sesame Street* crowd.

"We'll see," I said noncommittally.

I thanked Mallory and left. As I walked down the path two things happened.

Loud, jarring notes crashed out the window—along with happy shrieks of "Sweet Georgia brownies!"

I stopped, stunned. I'd got through to Randall. Sharing my feelings about music had worked. I felt pretty good about that.

The rhododendrons rustled violently.

These were the rhododendrons beside the window, the ones that shook while I played. I'd thought my loudness and jumping got them going. I was wrong.

A man pushed his way out of the big purple flowers. The man from the photograph. Mallory's husband.

He was holding hedge clippers. He pointed their sharp—head-chopping sharp—blades at me. "You. Piano player. We need to talk."

I panicked. Gerald Sherman must know I had a crush on his wife.

Like Mallory said, the guy was intense. Which made me stupid.

I ran.

Chapter Nine

I wasn't proud of my reaction. I was still brooding about my less-than-manly behaviour when I arrived at the Keynote the next morning. I'd texted Constable Barker that I wanted to talk to him about the case. He replied that he'd be in the conference room first thing in the morning. He would spare me some time if I got in early.

In the lobby, the burly security guard was lounging back in his chair. I noticed a gold watch gleaming on his wrist beside the smart watch. He kept stretching out his arm to admire the new watch.

I rode the elevator up. Mike was in his office, on the phone. He beckoned me in. "Excuse me for a moment, Mr. Mayor," he said. Lowering the phone, he gestured to an espresso machine. "Help yourself, Rocker Crocker." Winking, Mike lifted the phone again. "Sorry, Your Worship. I was just greeting an important colleague."

I glowed. Mike Dante, interrupting the mayor of Vancouver for me. I walked with executive-type confidence over to the espresso machine. I picked up one of the tiny cups beside it. I imagined future interrupted phone conversations. *Give me a minute, would you, Mr. Prime Minister? Nate Crocker just made the scene.*

I held the tiny cup under the machine's spigot. I'd never tasted espresso before. I was more of a hot chocolate type of guy.

I pulled the spigot down. Dark liquid dribbled out—and stopped. That was it? I'd have to tell Mike something was wrong with his machine.

"No, I don't get the protests, either," he said into the phone. "I find a new home for every person, every family, from the buildings I tear down. I don't want anyone out on the street. At Dante Enterprises, we care about people.

"…What's that, Your Worship? Well, it's a democracy. People have the right to protest. And we welcome them to the Keynote. We welcome everyone. That's the Dante way. That's the Dante *image*."

Since there wasn't much liquid in the tiny cup, I downed it all at once. And promptly spluttered it back up. What *was* this stuff?

"Now, about my donation for a new playground," Mike was saying.

I headed to the conference room. Constable Barker was frowning at a laptop screen. On seeing me he pushed a box of doughnuts across the table.

"Thanks," I said as I reached for a chocolate-glazed one. I took a huge bite to nuke the lingering taste of espresso.

"You should become a cop," the constable remarked. "You have the two main qualifications: you want to solve cases and you like doughnuts."

Mike's jolly voice boomed into my mind: *I see a long, prosperous business relationship ahead of us.* That was my career goal, to make it big through Dante Enterprises.

I didn't say this. I didn't want to throw shade on what the constable did for a living. Instead I told him about my musical-chairs, musical-victims theory. I finished up with, "The fourth Beethoven was focused only on one victim. Like a savvy musical-chairs player would focus only on the centre chairs."

The constable didn't dismiss my theory or look at me oddly. Instead he got the pleased look of a teacher listening to a prize student. It was not the look teachers generally gave me. I was the kid who drummed out tunes on desks.

Barker said, "It's a real possibility that the thief targeted you and Zandi as distractions. That Susan Volker was the intended target."

He turned his laptop toward me. Two red blobs shone off the screen. I looked closer. Rubies, set in gold.

"Susan Volker's earrings," Constable Barker explained. "Worth thousands. It could be just a coincidence. But I don't believe in coincidences."

To me the rubies had zero appeal. If I

were Susan Volker, I'd use them as stop signs, not ear bling. I didn't get the point of jewelry. Unlike the guard downstairs, gawking at his flashy gold watch.

Constable Barker shut his laptop. "I like that you've thought about this, shared your ideas."

"Don't forget about the thief's knuckle-cracking," I reminded him.

"Oh, right." Barker reached for his cell, punched in a number. "Thanks for coming by, Nate."

Though friendly, his message was unmistakable. This episode of *Nate Crocker, Amateur Detective* was over. From now on the pros would take charge.

I walked out slowly. I wasn't offended. I liked the constable. But he needed to take the knuckle-cracking more seriously.

As I shut the door behind me, I heard him say into his phone, "Our thief has likely sold the rubies by now… Yeah, exactly. We watch out for somebody who suddenly has a lot of cash."

I got on the elevator. As it *whish*-ed me

down to the lobby I thought about being alert for someone with extra cash.

The doors opened on the lobby—and the guard, admiring his gold watch.

I couldn't pass the security desk without a look at that watch to see if it was worth its weight in rubies.

Mike was a good guy. He'd given me an opportunity other teen musicians only dreamed of. He deserved to know if a thief was working for him.

The guard was reading a golf magazine. Pistachio shells covered the counter. He brushed some out of the way, onto the floor. The old let-the-cleaning-staff-deal-with-it approach, like Charlie's Chicken customers sticking chewed gum on their plates.

But being an inconsiderate slob didn't make you a thief.

I leaned over the counter for a look at his watch and—wowzers. Like I said, I'm not into bling. But even I recognized the brand name on the watch face. Rolex. Equal to about six months of what Mom paid in rent.

I needed to get him to talk. "Nice watch. It goes well with…" *With the smart watch straining around your big wrist on a band about to snap.* "…with your Keynote uniform," I finished. "I wouldn't mind a watch like that."

Sladen chortled. "Dream on, kid. My advice? Get a stick, shove it in the ground and see which way the sun falls. That's more your budget."

"Hahahaha," I fake-laughed. "So, Mike must pay you well."

At that the guard flinched. He looked a little scared. Then his face hardened. Maybe he was remembering that compared to him I was the size of a gnat. He opened his mouth to snarl out a reply. Instead I heard:

"Mamma mia, here I go again!"

It was his phone. He was into ABBA? As I gaped at him in horror, the guard said, "Yes, Mr. Dante, he's right here. Will do."

He tapped his phone off. "The boss wants you out there performing. Like *now*."

"Sure," I said. I realized it wasn't me the guard had been afraid of. It was my asking how he could afford the watch.

At the piano I hunkered down and started a quiet, slow version of "Ode to Joy." The volume, the jumping around, could wait. I needed to think.

Across the courtyard Zandi and her buddies were shouting. "Want to develop something, Mike Dante? Try a heart!"

I fit their words to the ode music and sang along. "Try a heart, oh try a heart, oh try a heart, oh *tryyyy* a heart…" But it wasn't hearts I was thinking about. It was wigs and scowling masks. Frilly shirts and black pants.

I was almost sure the guard was the fourth Beethoven. Which brought me back to the question of the costume. The outfits Beethovens One, Two and Three wore wouldn't fit. I had to find out the name of the costume company. Ask if they'd suited one up in super-size.

"Super-size, oh super-size, oh super-size, oh *suuuu*-per-size," I crooned.

The Fifth Beethoven

Forget asking Beethovens Two and Three. They'd knock on their foreheads. Idiots. Ask a simple question.

Mike's assistant, Trish Laharne, could tell me. But if I asked Laharne, she might mention it to Mike. Until I could present him with solid proof, Mike shouldn't know I was snooping.

I paused, thinking, holding down the final middle C of the ode way too long. For now I'd shelve the costume company lead. There had to be another way to find out about the guard. Sure, I could just let the police handle it. But I kept remembering Mike's frustration about the thefts happening on his property. No. I would solve this for him. He'd given me a break. I owed him. And I wanted to impress him, to see his grateful smile, the approval shining out of his bright blue eyes.

But in my mind something else shone. The gold of the guard's Rolex, glowing brighter, taunting me. Without the name of the costume company I couldn't prove the guard was the fourth Beethoven.

Nein, nein, Nate! The one, the only, the real Ludwig van Beethoven draped over the piano, scowling at me. And I realized, bah-bah-bah-*boom!*, I was wrong. I did have another way to check out the guard. The thief was someone who knew Susan Volker. Constable Barker agreed me on with that. Now I saw what to do: Plan B, for (fake) Beethoven.

The real Beethoven kept scowling. He mentally texted, *You going to play that middle C till you collect your old-age pension?*

Fine. I switched to the *Fifth*'s opening notes, and then he vanished.

I played fast and loud right up to my break. The crowd loved it. Mike, strolling past, grinned and saluted me. I grinned back. My boss was pleased with me now. Wait till I unmasked the fourth Beethoven. Wait till I executed Plan B.

Chapter Ten

First order of business: a phone call. I couldn't make the call in the courtyard. I'd have to yell to be heard—and I wanted to keep Plan B confidential. Couldn't make it in the lobby either. The guard might eavesdrop. Not that a King Kong-like guy seemed capable of stealth, but you never knew.

I opted for the shelter of the news vendor's kiosk. He had no customers at the moment. And the vendor was wearing earbuds. Whatever he was listening to, it made him smile. Noticing me he took one earbud out. "Can I help you?"

"No, thanks."

The smile disappeared. "Of course. A read-and-run." He popped the earbud back in.

I punched in Constable Barker's number. "The guard. He's our thief. *He's wearing a Rolex*," I said when he answered.

A brief silence. The constable in awe at my detective work, I figured. Then:

"Who *is* this?"

He cut off my attempt to reply with a kind, if weary, "Ah, of course. Crocker. I should have known. Listen, son. We're checking into the guard. Did you hear that? I said *we're* checking into him. As in, you're not."

"But shouldn't you arrest him? Like, right now? He's—"

"Crocker, enough."

"But—"

"I like that you want to solve this. And I do think you should consider becoming a cop—when you're twenty-one. Also, that'll put me close to retirement."

"Oh, hahaha."

"A little constabulary humour. Here, I'll tell you how you *can* get involved."

I brightened. "A stake-out?"

"You could join your local neibourhood Junior Block Watch association," Barker said. "With other good-citizen kids, you can rake leaves for the elderly and infirm, take out their garbage, stuff like that. Once a month, a cop like myself comes by to talk to the Juniors. And, hey, there's no cop meeting without doughnuts!"

I let this suggestion fall to the silent death it deserved. The constable hadn't taken the knuckle-cracking seriously. Now he was ignoring the Rolex, which to me blazed *mystery solved* in neon letters.

I let out a loud, gusty sigh. "Sure. Always look forward to doughnuts."

"So you'll leave the case to us?"

I tapped my phone screen several times. "Bad connection, sir. See you." I hung up.

The vendor was straightening magazines. He still had the earbuds in.

I thought of his bitter read-and-run remark and felt sorry for him. I fished out some money for a roll of mints. After all, Plan B involved interviewing a witness. Better not to alienate them with onion breath.

The vendor removed an earbud and took the money. "Don't mind me listening to my

Tending to Your Tulips podcast. I have to. If I don't, I hear horrible things." He shuddered.

I wondered what he meant. People swearing, probably. Whatever it was, I had more important things to think about. The constable refused to listen to me about the guard. I'd have to carry out Plan B on my own.

Zandi was sitting on a bench not far from the newspaper kiosk. While her friends waved signs and shouted, she handed out flyers—that is, she *tried* to hand out the flyers. Most people were in the usual necks-craned-up mode, gawking at the Keynote.

Today's flyer read: *Homes aren't only for the wealthy. Stop Mike Dante!* plus a list of Dante Enterprises' developments.

Zandi frowned at me. Her usual greeting, in other words.

I hesitated. I couldn't think of a less likely person to ask for help. Still, desperate circumstances called for desperate measures.

I said, "Want to get your stolen stuff back? I have a plan. I could use your help with one small detail."

I told Zandi my theory about Sladen the guard being the fourth Beethoven. I filled her in on Plan B. She cooperated. She accompanied me to the lobby. She fake-smiled as I snapped photos. All part of the plan.

She wasn't so cooperative about following my other instructions, to avoid looking at the security guard's Rolex. "I'm curious," she defended herself. "I've never seen a Rolex in real life."

I made throat-slitting gestures to signal her to stop. The guard was sitting at reception, reading a golf magazine. He might overhear.

I took more photos. Oh, man. Her eyes went Rolex-ward again. I should have enlisted a garden gnome, not Zandi.

Elevator doors opened. The guard dropped his magazine, sat up straight. Mike stepped out. He looked from me to Zandi. Winked at me.

I did my own fake smile back. I didn't like deceiving him. When all this was over, I'd explain.

To Zandi I called, "How about a side view, er, honey. Profile shot. And remember: eyes on me, not the—not anything else."

"Of course…honey."

The guard watched Mike leave. He waited till the boss was halfway across the courtyard. Then he picked up his magazine and sat back in his chair.

Zandi and I wrapped up our photo shoot with, surprise, surprise, a disagreement. "I want in on the rest of your Plan B," she murmured as we passed the guard. "It's my file. It should be my plan as much as yours. Victim's rights."

I couldn't imagine being anxious about a file of how-to-protest instructions. Maybe she was saying this to be annoying. Annoying was Zandi's second nature.

I tried a new strategy: being patient. "Safer not to get involved," I advised. "Barker told me to lay off the guard. I could get into a lot of trouble. No point in you taking risks, too."

"Yeah, I'm not buying the spare-the-helpless-damsel thing, Crocker. You're not sidelining me. I'm coming along." She glared.

I glared back. So much for patience. I'd product-tested it with Zandi and could now rule out ever trying it again. Waste of energy.

"Forget it. What you're talking about isn't victim's rights. It's victim's dumbness." I wheeled around and made for the piano.

It was a relief to play my next set. Why couldn't life be like music? With music, people heard you. The real you. No misunderstanding, no pretending.

I played past the end of my shift. Mike strolled past, waved at the crowd, clapped along with them. When I finished he grinned. "I guess I'm going to have to pay you overtime, Rocker Crocker."

"No, sir. That's not—I mean, I kept playing because I liked being in the music. I wanted to stay there."

An idiotic utterance. But Mike studied me in that way he had. He nodded, patted my shoulder. "The humdrum isn't for me, either. You keep playing the way you do and things will open up for you at Dante Enterprises."

"Yes, sir. I mean, yes, Mike."

He laughed. I relaxed. He saw my potential, not my idiocy. I remembered his frustration that the thefts had happened on his property. *Wait till I unmask the fourth Beethoven*, I thought for the thousand-and-first time. *It will be my thanks to him*.

Two older ladies came up to Mike, giggling and asking for his autograph. All those cheerful commercials made him a celebrity. I stuffed my sheet music in my backpack. I closed and locked up the piano.

Zandi was on her bench, surrounded by her protest buddies. Maybe they were planning new ways to holler and wave signs. Let them. With Zandi busy, I could execute Plan B on my own.

I adopted a pest-avoidance strategy: a crouch-and-run to the bus shelter. From his kiosk the news vendor shot me a weird look.

The West Vancouver bus pulled up. I boarded, pressed my transit card against the sensor and strode to the back of the bus. Plopping my backpack beside me, I sat down and refreshed Susan Volker's address on my phone. I hoped she'd be home. I didn't want to risk phoning ahead. The last thing I needed was Susan checking with Constable Barker. I could just hear Barker's voice blasting at me: *Crocker, don't you dare approach a police witness!*

The bus wound through the Stanley Park forest, then up over Lions Gate Bridge. At the sight of the North Shore mountains ahead, of the sun-sparkling Burrard Inlet below, I relaxed. Plan B for (fake) Beethoven was a cinch. All I had to do was show Susan Volker the photos I'd taken in the lobby.

Of Sladen the security guard, needless to say. Not Zandi the protest pest. Zandi had provided cover as my pretend girlfriend, but I'd been snapping Sladen, front and profiles.

Zandi as a girlfriend. I couldn't imagine it. A person would go crazy.

The bus glided along the bridge. It was fun to be sailing over Lions Gate, leaving downtown behind. Being Zandi-free.

"Hi Nate."

No. No, it couldn't be.

But it was. Zandi stood over me, smiling. Not just her usual scornful smile. This one had *gotcha!* in it. She moved my backpack to one side and sat down beside me.

Chapter Eleven

Zandi was determined, I had to give her that. Not that I said so. For the rest of the bus ride I sat in fuming silence. Which I could tell she enjoyed.

"Thanks so much...*honey*," Zandi chirped, as I helped her out at the bus stop. No, I didn't want her company. But she was limping, and I thought she might twist her bad ankle coming down the bus steps.

After a while Zandi wasn't quite as chirpy. Susan Volker's was your typical West Van house, many blocks up a steep hill. The street names got alphabetically higher along with the altitude. The more we trekked, the worse Zandi limped. By Gordon Avenue she was panting. By Jefferson she was stopping for breaks.

But she didn't complain. Not once. I had to give her that, too.

It did cross my calculating mind to run ahead. Susan Volker lived on Ottawa Avenue. I could be finished with Susan Volker and Zandi would be still be wilting, if not fainted dead away, at an L or M street.

I didn't. I settled for giving her a Beethoven-worthy scowl. Not because I was angry. Because I admired her, grudgingly.

"So what's in this all-important file?" I demanded. "It can't just be about protests. Let me guess: you keep a diary in it, full of girlish confidences. Your dreams of one day meeting, let's see…Robert Pattinson."

Zandi was kneeling, massaging her ankle. Now, staggering to her feet, she raised her bad ankle and clasped it in her right hand. "I don't need your insults, Crocker. And the file is *all* about housing. Being a toady to Mike Dante, you wouldn't understand."

Nose in the air, she hopped up to Haywood Avenue. I followed, thinking I should be insulted by the word *toady*. But instead I wanted to laugh at the sight of Zandi hopping.

Turning a potential laugh into a cough, I caught up with her and put an arm across her shoulders. "I know. Let's be positive and fun about this. We'll pretend we're in a three-legged race."

She gave me the most suspicious side-long glance I'd seen yet. But I kept a straight face. So, hopping was how we arrived at Susan Volker's place on Ottawa Avenue.

Zandi pointed. "What is *that*?"

"That's what we call a detached house."

"I meant the police car," she said icily.

Susan Volker's driveway extended along the side of her house. In the driveway we saw a shining red Mercedes. And a black-and-white copmobile.

Zandi gulped. "Wow. Barker's good."

I shuffled us a few feet closer for a better view. "That's not Barker. The car has the West Van police crest. Listen. We've hobbled this far. We hobble on." I said.

This was impatience talking. Even if a West Van crony of Barker's was waiting with handcuffs, I was going to flash the guard's photo at Susan.

On the porch, Zandi sank into a white wrought-iron chair. I crashed the lion's head knocker against the door. The lion's lips were curled into a snarl, almost a treble-clef shape. Intrigued, I tried to curl my mouth up the same way.

The door opened on a whiff of coconut perfume. "My goodness, how unfriendly!" exclaimed Susan Volker.

"Sorry, ma'am. I was just, er, exercising my facial muscles. I'm with Dante Enterprises. I have a photo to show you. Of a man."

I stumbled on, my plan to win Susan's trust with smooth dialogue in shreds. "We wondered if you knew this one guy—that is, we're interested in helping you. I mean, if *you're* interested in—"

"Stop blathering and show me," Susan Volker interrupted, not unkindly.

I handed my phone to her. "There's more than one photo. You just swipe..." I made waving gestures. You never knew how tech-savvy older folks were. Even Mom texted with—get this—a *forefinger*.

Swiping back and forth, Susan broke into a delighted smile. "I do know him. Yes, indeed."

With difficulty I kept my jaw from thudding to my chest. I was right! I, Nate Crocker, had cracked the case. Not just in my imaginings, where it was easy to make theories work. In real life.

Sladen the guard and Susan were friends. Definitely more than acquaintances, the way she was smiling and swiping. Susan had told Sladen she was taking her rubies in for repair. Told him when and where and he'd used that knowledge.

Zandi raised a hand. We high-fived. I basked in her rare un-sardonic smile—for three seconds.

Then: *Tell her*, Zandi mouthed.

Oh, right. I had to do the awkward thing, be the spoiler. Sladen had stolen the rubies from Susan. Now, one Rolex later, he needed unmasking. No matter how much Susan liked him I had to do it.

I said, "About the guy in the photos. He knew about the rubies."

"Of course he did! I told him when we met. And now the shy thing has sent you as a love messenger." Susan clasped my phone to her heart and blushed.

This time my jaw did plummet. I was powerless to control it. King Kong-like Sladen, a shy thing. Me, a love messenger. None of it made sense. Zandi and I hadn't just got off the bus in a different 'hood. We were on a different planet.

Zandi stood up. She put a hand under my jaw and shoved it back in place. To Susan she said, "Sorry, we're a bit confused. When did you meet the security guard?"

Susan shuddered. "It was after that horrid thief in the Beethoven costume stole my purse. I was in the courtyard, too shocked and upset to move."

Also too busy screaming, as I recalled.

"People were asking me if I wanted an ambulance. An ambulance! What idiots. 'I can't wear *ambulances* in my ears,' I said. 'It's my rubies I want back.'"

She gave a deep, blissful sigh. "Then the Keynote security guard appeared. He picked me up in his strong arms, carried me into the lobby and brought me water. He couldn't have been nicer. I quite fancied him," she said with a giggle. "And now he's sent you! I knew there was chemistry between us. I just knew it."

Zandi looked at me. Her eyes were bright, her mouth trembling. She found this *funny*.

I let out a long, low moan, leaned my forehead against the door frame and closed my eyes. "Please, ma'am. Help my last remaining minuscule brain cell understand this. You only met King Ko—I mean, Sladen, after the robbery."

"Of course! That's what I just told you." Susan's voice turned worried. "You seem unwell, young man. Can I get you something?"

A live lion to devour me, I thought. It would be less painful than this. So much for my detective abilities, for Nate Crocker, Amateur Sleuth. More like Nate Crocker, Professional Moron.

I forced myself to face Susan again. For one thing she had my phone. I held my hand out and she returned it. Great. The phone now smelled of coconut perfume.

"Did you tell anyone you were taking your earrings in for repair?" I asked.

"Just my son."

Her son, huh? Maybe this visit wasn't the disaster I'd thought. Zandi and I traded glances. I imagined some spoiled West Van kid, surly that his allowance didn't exceed five hundred a week. Could Susan Volker's son be the fourth Beethoven? Hmm. The plot thickened.

Only to thin right out again.

Susan beamed, "That's my son's car by the sidewalk. He's a police officer. He stopped by a few minutes ago for a tea-and-cookies break. Would you like to meet him? I'd be happy to—wait, where are you two going? And what's with the three-legged racing?"

Chapter Twelve

The next morning I removed the cover from the piano. But instead of playing I collapsed on the bench and sank my face into my hands. I'd been so sure that the guard knew Susan, knew she'd be taking her rubies in for repair. It had seemed as simple as ABC:

The security guard sported a Rolex.

The thief knew Susan Volker would be carrying rubies around.

Therefore, the guard, someone Susan knew, was the thief.

But I'd scored an F in my ABCs.

Alphabet letters spun in my brain. I'd failed. So much for my dream of finding the fourth Beethoven.

"Hi Nate. You look like you have a massive headache."

It was Zandi. I lifted my face. "I *am* a massive headache," I informed her.

She gave a half-smile that was part kind, part exasperated. "You had a good theory, Crocker. I don't think you should give up because of one mistake. You should keep trying."

I stared. Zandi, being sympathetic. Being *nice*. Maybe we were finally friends. I could use a friend today. "I appreciate the encouragement," I said weakly. "Uh, do you want to catch a burger later?"

"What I want to catch is my missing file." Zandi limped off to her bench to hand out flyers.

So much for friendliness. But my feelings weren't hurt. I was used to the chip on Zandi's shoulder. Instead I was curious. What was with this file? Zandi was practically hopping with anxiety to get it back. (Correction: she was literally hopping.) Zandi claimed the contents involved the *Give Us Back Our Homes!* protests. I didn't believe that for a 32nd-note beat. The file had to be personal.

The Fifth Beethoven

I lifted the fallboard and began tinkling out "Ode to Joy." I surveyed the protesters near Zandi, waving signs and yelling. One protester was tall and broad-shouldered. A single dark curl of hair drooped down his forehead, Superman-style. How many hours and how much hair gel had that taken?

Irritated, I played louder. After a while I realized I hadn't propped up the sheet music. I didn't need it. I knew this baby. Which made me think I might be ready for the real sheet music, not the easy version. The real music was in the key of D minor, not the easier G that I was rocking out now.

D...G...More letters in my brain. But they weren't spinning now. I was rethinking them. Like Zandi said, I'd made a mistake. Unmasking the fourth Beethoven hadn't turned out to be as simple as ABC. But that didn't mean I should toss all the letters out.

A: Sladen had a Rolex, true. And like Barker, I believed B: the thief knew Susan would be carting rubies around. Out with C, though: Sladen hadn't actually met Susan until after the robbery.

I sang along with the music, "Dah dah dah dah DAH dah dah!" Time to take my old idea out again. The one about finding the company that made the Beethoven costumes. Asking if they'd rented one in super-size.

This time I would find out the company name. Beethovens Two and Three could crack all the jokes they wanted; *I* was going to crack the case. They couldn't stop me. No one could. And Mike would be impressed with my initiative.The thought lit me up. I played "Ode to Joy" even louder, even faster, a rocking staccato.

Knock, knock! Someone was rapping on the piano top in time with the beat. I looked up and saw Mike smiling at me. A crowd formed, clapped along with my playing and Mike's knocking.

When I finished, Mike dropped a couple of twenties in my cap, winked at me. With a wave to the cheering crowd, he strode off.

Sweat ran into my eyes. The crowd blurred. I was perspiring like a waterfall and hadn't even realized it.

The scent of mango floated nearby. "Here, Nate. Tissues for you."

I took them and wiped my eyes and fore-head. Now I could see Mallory Sherman's green gaze, her wide smile, her long, dark-red hair. "Thanks," I gulped.

I wanted to add something suave. On my own it was easy to think of clever, witty remarks. In her presence my brain packed up and left.

The tissues in my hand were dripping. "Guess I better bring a cloth next time," I joked feebly. "Or maybe a beach towel."

"Pow, pow!" squealed Randall. I hadn't noticed the kid till now. He punched the side of the piano over and over. His way of imitating Mike.

Mallory pulled Randall away before he could splinter the wood. With an apologetic smile she tried her own joke. "Opportunity knocks, you could say. A couple of moms have asked if you'd like to play at their kids' parties."

Absolutely not. *No*. Just say it, Crocker.

"I—I'll let you know," I said.

"Sure," she smiled.

If words failed me, music never did. I started in on Randall's favourite, "Sweet Georgia Brown." In no time the kid was jumping side to side and waving his arms in circles. The kids in the crowd imitated him. Soon I was surrounded by miniature human windmills. Finishing up "Georgia," I gestured to them. "The energy source of the future!"

The crowd howled. They kept clapping, and the kids kept windmilling their arms. When some of the little windmills collapsed, worn out, against their parents, Randall climbed on top of the piano. The jangle of the keys he used as a foothold silenced the crowd.

Mallory looked uncertain. I shrugged at her and grinned. Randall the scene-stealer. I was fine with it.

Randall frowned around at everyone. A deep, menacing frown I'd seen somewhere before. Of course! His dad.

The kid leaned forward. Started—get this—lecturing the crowd. "Music, the really good music, is about nobody-can-make-me. Composers are the giant."

The giant? Ohhh, he meant *defiant*. I bit the inside of my cheeks to avoid laughing.

With his little voice, only the people at the front could hear. But everyone watched, fascinated. Randall ploughed on: "No matter how people try to talk them out of it, these giants create their own sound." He stopped and took a bow.

Awe replaced my urge to laugh. I looked at Mallory. "That's almost word for word what I'd said to him at his birthday party."

"Yes," said Mallory. "He often does that."

What a memory. When he got older, Randall was going to kill at exam time—without any need to study.

His mom lifted him off the piano. Randall looked solemnly at me, curled his fingers and bashed imaginary keys. I took that to mean he was still playing his piano. I nodded back solemnly. I liked that I'd inspired him. That I'd been his opportunity knock.

Instead of launching into another tune I tinkled out more "Georgia" notes. I was thinking. There were knocks of opportunity—and knocks of stupidity. Like Beethovens Two and Three knocking on their foreheads when I asked for the name of the costume company. A simple question. Why be idiots? Why make it complicated?

"Georgia named her, Georgia claimed her," I sang, then signalled for Randall to finish it off.

"Sweet Georgia brownies!" he yelled.

Smart kid. Unlike Bo Dante's buddies. *Why make a simple question complicated?*

People clapped and whistled. Randall took bows. Not me. I was thinking some more.*Knock, knock.*

Who's there?

Knocks!

"Bah-bah-bah-*boom!*" I yelled.

Because now I knew the name of the costume company. Beethovens Two and Three had told it to me, after all. Simple question, simple answer.

Chapter Thirteen

Two o'clock rolled around. End of shift. I surveyed the courtyard. No Zandi. Had she given up protesting? Where were pests when you needed them?

A Beethoven strolled by. He waved and I waved back, though I wasn't sure which Beethoven it was. Then he yawned. The giveaway. It was Bo Dante. No doubt the night sailor was heading up to his dad's office for a quiet nap.

Quiet. The word nudged my brain. Zandi, saying how much noise I made. That with me around nobody noticed the protesters. *They went to a park down the street where it's quieter.*

I knew the park. A small one, by a cathedral. I walked over. On seeing me, the protesters waved their signs and shouted, "Down with Dante Enterprises!" Though I noticed the guy with the forehead curl didn't move around as much. Worried about disturbing his gelled 'do, I figured.

Unable to stand with the others, Zandi was sitting on a step. I thought of the thief slamming her to the ground. It would be so satisfying to hear the *click!* of handcuffs closing around his big wrists.

I sat down beside her. "Want to go somewhere?"

"With *you?*"

I gestured to the guy with the curl. "Superman is busy. Besides, you'll be interested in the place I'm thinking of."

The protester nearest us overheard. She giggled. "Oooo, Zandi has a date."

"Aren't there some lost marbles you should be looking for?" I asked. Turning away, I told Zandi about the costume company.

"And you want me to come with you on another little sleuthing adventure." She sounded skeptical. But not uninterested.

I nodded. "The principle of distraction. It worked for the thief; it'll work for us. While you grab people's attention, I'll snoop around."

"'Grab attention.' I'm supposed to what, do cartwheels?"

"Just be your normal annoying self. If I'm right about the security guard, we might find your missing file."

File. I'd said the magic word. Her dark eyes widened. "Sure, I'll go with you. Thanks for asking me along. Though I still think your distract-and-snoop idea is half-baked."

"No, it's cooked right through," I assured her.

The nearby protester giggled again. "Ooo. You two are so cute!"

I helped Zandi up. I glanced again at the guy with the curl. He smiled at us. Amazing he could. With that amount of gel on his head you'd think he'd have a headache.

To the giggly protester I said out of the side of my mouth, "Hot stock investment tip for you."

"Oooo, what?"

"Hair gel."

"Why are you being so hostile about Darren?" Zandi demanded as we fast-tracked it—in her case, fast-hopped it—to the bus stop.

"His name's Darren? Oooo."

A bus ride to Main Street and we saw Superman again. Except this time he was painted on a wall along with Spiderman, Darth Vader, a green-faced witch and various clowns.

And on top of the building, in big red letters, the sign:

Knox Costume Company.

As we reached the front door it swung open. People in costumes piled out, laughing and chatting. They surged across the street to a place called Tony's Sports Bar.

"Wait," I said.

"About to close. Holiday weekend," Prince Charles called back.

Zandi shut her eyes and swayed, seeming about to faint. I put an arm around her. "You okay?"

She grimaced. "I was until Aladdin stepped on my bad ankle."

I pushed the door open into the lobby. An arctic blast hit us. Talk about industrial-strength AC.

No receptionist, unless you counted the giant plastic shark hanging from the ceiling. The shark leered at us through red-smeared teeth.

I helped Zandi to a chair. "I'll see what I can find out. Then I'm springing for a cab to take you home. Yes, I know, you're not a damsel in distress," I added as she started to protest. "But it's my fault you got that Aladdin foot-stomp."

I spotted vending machines down the hall. "And I'll get you a treat. How about a mocha with green licorice flavoring?"

She laughed. I, the enemy, made a joke and she laughed. "You're full of it, Crocker. Those machines wouldn't have anything so gruesome. But I appreciate the thought. I'd love a coffee. With cinnamon, if possible. No milk, no sugar. Definitely no green licorice."

"On its way," I promised. I glanced at the shark. His shiny glass eyes seemed to be sizing me up as his own snack preference.

I jogged down the hall, trying each door I passed. I was searching for someone, anyone, to ask about the fourth Beethoven costume. All doors were locked.

Then, just before the vending machines, one door stood open. Through it I saw a huge room with racks of costumes. On top of each rack was a sign with a letter: A for Aladdin, anteater, Aquaman. B for Batman...you get the idea. Along the wall by the door hung full-length mirrors, I guess for when people tried on costumes.

Across the room, a white rabbit tapped on a computer. The purse slung over the rabbit's shoulder told me it—she—was about to leave.

"Just a minute!" I called.

The rabbit turned, revealing a young woman's annoyed face under the long white ears.

I sprinted toward her. "Don't sign out. I need to check an order."

She squinted across the racks. She fumbled in her purse for a pair of glasses.

And I realized: when she got a proper look at me, she'd know I wasn't an employee.

I dived between the L and M racks. An Abraham Lincoln mask smiled kindly down at me. *I bet Honest Abe never trespassed*, I thought. I was making a habit of it this summer. First the Keynote, now Knox.

"Hello?" The rabbit sounded peevish.

I grabbed Abe's mask, slid it over my face. Pulled on his black jacket and stove-pipe hat. His black pants I didn't have time for.

I strolled over to the rabbit. "There's a customer in the lobby. Says she needs information."

"It's the long weekend. We're closing."

I nodded, hoping the stovepipe hat didn't fall off. "Yeah. But I thought we could help her out before we head over to the sports bar. Y'know, for a, uh, brew," I added, trying to talk like a twenty-something.

The rabbit turned to a series of video monitors. The top left screen showed Zandi sitting under the shark. "She doesn't look old enough to be a customer."

I made my voice whiny, like I was anxious to start my holiday weekend, too. "What was I supposed to do, card her?"

Heavy sigh. "Fine. What's the customer order number?"

"I—she didn't have it. She's from Dante Enterprises. Her company bought a fourth Beethoven costume, different size than the first three. That's what she wants to check on."

The rabbit tapped on her keyboard. Rabbit ears wagging, she skimmed the text on the screen. "That's correct. First three sizes were medium. Fourth was...my goodness, we don't get many requests for that size in Beethoven."

I let out a whoop. I'd been right. The security guard was the fourth Beethoven. I'd cracked the case like he cracked pistachio nuts. Wait till I dazzled Mike Dante with my detective work.

The Fifth Beethoven

The rabbit sniffed. "I don't know why you're so excited. We do special orders all the time. Had a seven-foot-tall client in here just today. I'll print off the Dante order; you give it to the young woman. And show her out. As of this minute I'm off-duty."

The printer beside her churned out a piece of paper. She whipped it off the tray and then slapped it on the counter.

I picked it up and saw those wonderful words: *specialty size*. Gotcha, fourth Beethoven.

Then I frowned. The date on the order was several weeks back. Had Sladen known ahead when Susan Volker, someone he'd never met, would be carrying rubies?

I rolled up the paper and slapped it against the palm of my hand. Of course he hadn't. Dante Enterprises bought a costume for him in case one of the other Beethovens got sick. That was it. The fourth costume was so Sladen could fill in. Except that's not what he had used it for. As Mike had said the first day we met, *What a world, huh?*

The rabbit was signing out of her computer. "I thought you were still on sick leave, Henry."

"Er…" Some dude named Henry usually wore the Honest Abe costume. And Henry had been sick. I shrugged that off. "A couple of aspirin and I was fine."

"A couple of aspirin…for a *motorcycle accident*? I heard you zoomed straight into a wall, broke all kinds of bones."

She put her glasses back in her purse. I ran between two racks and hid. I couldn't fake being Henry any longer. I hoped when I got my licence I'd be a better driver.

"Henry, you still here? We can walk over to Tony's together."

Sliding under some ballet tutus, I removed the stovepipe hat and Abe mask. No wonder Knox had the air conditioning on at full blast. These costumes got hot.

"Henry? Did you not wait?" With a *tsk* of annoyance the white rabbit left the room. The door slammed.

Now I could go find Zandi and show her the order. As I returned the Abe costume to the L rack, I pictured Zandi's admiring, scorn-free gaze. *Wow, Crocker. You solved the mystery of the fourth Beethoven! I'm so impressed*.

Like Zandi would ever, ever say that.

I tried opening the door. Couldn't. A small oval screen was waiting for a keycard swipe.

I was locked in. Trapped. With a three-day weekend stretching before me.

Chapter Fourteen

I know, I know. I had my phone. But calling for help would mean I'd be caught trespassing. I doubted the folks at Knox Costumes would be as forgiving as Mike Dante.

The rabbit would be back Tuesday morning. Once the door opened I would dash out.

I could survive until then. I had water in my backpack plus a package of green licorice. And if I got really hungry, hey, this was a costume room. There had to be shoe leather around.

What bothered me was the thought of Zandi waiting, wondering where I was. Thinking I'd forgotten about her. When it was just the opposite. I did remember, right down to what she liked in her coffee.

She wouldn't know that. She'd assume I just walked off. I took out my phone. I didn't know her number, only her last name. I searched Canada411. I searched Instagram, Snapchat, Tiktok. Too many hits. I'd wear down my battery checking all of them.

Maybe she'd look me up. There's not so many Crockers. Yeah, do that, Zandi. Look up Crocker. I watched my phone, willing her to call.

She didn't. I punched into phone settings. My current voicemail greeting was me shouting, "Bah-bah-bah-*boom!*" I reset it to:

"This is for Zandi. Er, hi Zandi. I know you think that I just took off. I didn't. I was—I got trapped. If I ever get out of here and don't have to serve ti—I mean, I hope you'll give me another—another—"

Something tickled my nostrils. I looked down. I was beside a lemon costume. From the dust on the yellow shoulders, I was guessing not many people rented it.

I finished my message to Zandi with

a sneeze. Let's face it. I would always be short on suave.

I then left a message for Mom that I'd be home late. I didn't add, *three days late*. I didn't know how to explain that yet.

With nothing else to do, I wandered back to the B rack. Ballet tutus, Bambi, Batman—and there was Ludwig. The same mask, same costume I'd seen on Beethovens One to Four.

I lifted it off the rack. What the heck. I had hours to burn. I dropped my backpack, pulled on the frilly white shirt, the wig, the mask. Now to walk over to the mirrors and look at me, the fifth Beethoven.

At least, that was the plan. A crash of metal put a stop to it.

In the doorway a man in overalls stood beside an overturned pail. Sudsy water pooled around him.

He picked up his mop and jabbed it at me. "You gave me a scare. I wasn't expecting anyone to be here."

"Sorry. I was just heading to the sports bar. To join the others for a, y'know, brew."

"We don't have any Beethovens on staff, wise guy. You don't work at Knox. *What are you doing here?*"

I grabbed my backpack and ducked. Staying low, I ran to the end of the L rack. A lynx mask jutted up from the last hanger. Fitting my Beethoven-masked face into the lynx mask, I watched through two sets of eye slits.

The custodian was stomping along the other end of the racks. He still had his arm stretched out. But he wasn't holding a mop now.

It was a cell phone. He planned to snap my photo.

If he did, I'd be shamed all over social media. *Teenage felon breaks into costume company*. My chance of any career—dishwasher, let alone musician—would be, to put it in Beethoven's native language, *kaput*.

Except he'd seen the Beethoven mask, not me. Wait. That was even worse. If I got caught as Beethoven, the police might connect me to the thefts.

I had to get out of there. I crept past the K, J and I racks. Stopped. Straight ahead was the door, propped open.

My instinct was to run for it. But crouched down I couldn't see or hear the custodian. He was paused somewhere, too. Waiting to Instagram me.

A diversion. Something to throw, make noise with. Fool him into thinking I was in another part of the room.

I glanced along the I rack. I is for igneous. A rock would do nicely.

No rock costume. However, I spotted two prongs sticking up. Horns on top of a mask. I is for impala.

I reached up, grasped the horns. Threw. The mask landed near the R's, horns clattering.

The custodian lumbered to the R's. I sped out the door, skidding in the water and almost falling. Zoomed down the hall.

No Zandi in the lobby. I pushed out the door.

I saw a bus pulling away—with Zandi at a window.

I charged after the bus. "Wait! C'mon, *wait!*" I shouted. The driver must have seen me in his side mirror. He didn't stop. Of course he didn't. This was a holiday weekend.

I slumped down on the bus shelter bench. No way to get hold of Zandi to explain, until the next time I saw her protesting. But I was a *now* type of person; I couldn't wait.

I reached into my backpack for the print-out of the special-size order. I secured it in a side pocket, away from my sweating water bottle. I rummaged for other papers I should keep moisture-free. Under the Beethoven costume I'd jammed in my pack I found the two free-dinner coupons for the soon-to-open Andante restaurant. Also Mike's note about how he was sending coupons to each of the thief's victims—*the least we can do*, he'd said. What a decent guy. That made me feel better.

Then I felt even better. Not at the thought of porterhouse steaks dripping with juice or other delectable menu items. It was the thought of coupons and theft victims.

Because now I knew how to find Zandi Singh.

Zandi was on her porch step, sketching. "Mind if I join you?" I greeted her.

She scowled. "I do mind. Go away."

"Thanks." I sat down beside her. Zandi's sketch-in-progress was a new version of the one Randall had kicked through. This one had kids sitting on branches in the trees outside the yellow apartment building. "That's really good," I said.

Zandi set her pencils down. "What, you're making nice after ditching me?"

"No. I mean, yes. I like the drawing, okay? I want to jump right into it and climb those trees."

I got a flicker of a pleased smile. Which she promptly shrugged off. "Drawing is a bonus of being a protester. I get to create pictures. I've always doodled, since I was little. It's a compulsion, maybe like you with music."

I grinned at her. "See? We're actually capable of talking. A refreshing change from the usual hostilities."

"What are you doing here?"

I handed her a coffee. "Fresh from the corner café. Cinnamon, no milk, no sugar, no green licorice. And I'm here to apologize. I didn't mean to abandon you."

Zandi didn't say anything. With a red pencil she coloured in an eave of the building in her drawing.

"I got your address from Ms. Laharne." *Anything you want, just ask Trish Laharne*, Mike had said that first day. "Laharne had your addy because of Mike sending Andante coupons to the fourth Beethoven's victims."

I didn't add that Laharne had assumed my call was a boy-girl thing. That Laharne had whinnied, *That's so sweet, Nate!*

"I told Laharne you and I are friends." I paused. Zandi kept colouring I continued. "From the frosty silence, I take it you don't feel that way. That we're friends, I mean."

She sipped her coffee. "Friends don't bail on friends at costume shops."

"I didn't bail. An Instagram-happy custodian was chasing me. I finally escaped, but only after accidentally stealing a Beethoven costume."

Zandi choked on her coffee. "How do you accidentally steal—never mind. It must be exhausting to be you."

"It is," I assured her. I took out the Beethoven mask, wig and frilly shirt. "Now I have to figure out a way to return these."

She took the shirt, held it up. "Nice. I like the detail in the ruffles. So, aside from your trespassing and theft at Knox, did you find out anything?"

I showed her the Dante Enterprises customer order. Skimming it, she defrosted into a smile. "Wow! You were right, Sherlock."

"Please. I've had enough identities today. But it's the proof we wanted. The security guard is the fourth Beethoven. I'll go to Mike, show him the order."

From a jeans pocket Zandi pulled out her glittery pink-chip phone. "Don't make the mistake I did. Don't risk losing evidence. Back it up." She snapped a photo of the order, handed me her phone. "Here. Text it to yourself."

I tapped in my number. I also registered what she'd said. "The file in your bag that the thief grabbed—was it some kind of evidence?"

"It was…" Zandi began, then stopped.

I leaned back against the stairs and looked up. She was right about the exhaustion of being me. Watching clouds float by was about all I had energy left for.

"Of course you won't tell me," I said. "I'm on Team Dante. I'm the enemy. Whatever that file is, I can't be trusted to know about it."

Something besides clouds floated above. A yellow balloon. From the second-storey balcony a little girl reached for it. A woman pulled her back, scolding, "I've told you, never go out here alone. You might fall!"

I caught the balloon, gave it to Zandi. "Cute kid, your sister. What's her name?"

Zandi spun the balloon in her fingers. "Ashley. But she's not my sister. She and her mom are one of the other two families living here."

The townhouse was cheerful, green with a white door and white trim. It was also kind of narrow. "*Three* families?"

She nodded. "Mike Dante owns these townhouses. He put us here. Everyone he forced out of our building six months ago lives on this block. From what we hear, the people renovicted to make room for the Keynote live in a similar row of townhouses. Crammed in like us."

I looked down the row of townhouses. Each was a different colour of fresh paint with white trim. Bright, bold and, yeah, cheerful. But if you stopped noticing the cheerfulness, you saw how the houses were squashed up like an accordion.

I thought of the plaque in the Keynote lobby. Mike's award for finding new homes for displaced renters.

My bewilderment must have showed. Zandi explained, "These aren't our permanent homes. Dante Enterprises is housing us here while they look for places we can move to. We still pay low rent, but we have way less space."

I looked at the apartment building in Zandi's drawing. It reminded me of my place: rambling, comfortable, surrounded by trees. I imagined living where every breath you exhaled would land on someone. No wonder the kid on the balcony had let her balloon go. Inside, it would get crushed.

"How long do you have to wait?" I demanded.

Zandi shrugged. "It's by lottery. The problem is, by the time Dante Enterprises finds something, people are so anxious to get out they'll take anything."

I believe in new beginnings, Mike had said. Some new beginning for these folks. I didn't get it. I'd believed Mike.

And I still believed him. He caught me trespassing, then gave me a new beginning. That's what he did for people.

I said, "I'm going to tell Mike about this. Bosses are big-picture guys. He doesn't know the details of what's happening here."

Zandi's face closed up again. "Of course he doesn't know the details. And after this I'm going to rent me a penthouse suite at the Keynote." She shoved the Beethoven shirt back at me.

I stuffed it and the mask into my backpack. "See you," I said. "Pardon me—you and that massive chip on your shoulder."

Chapter Fifteen

I walked away. So much for my intention of making Zandi see I wasn't a bad guy. Impatient people shouldn't have intentions, obviously. Intentions take too much work.

I was sure Zandi was wrong about Mike. Sure he didn't know about the accordion-style accommodations. Once he did, he'd straighten things out.

All the same, I felt nervous. It wasn't my place to confront Mike about his business practices. But what I'd seen here, the families crammed in, wasn't fair. I had to tell him. It was the right thing to do. Why did doing the right thing have to be so difficult?

Maybe I should just get it over with, I thought. In my phone contacts I looked up Ms. Laharne's number. I'd leave a message asking her to have Mike call me. Explain that it was important.

Her cheery voice kicked in. "Dante Enterprises. Mr. Dante's office. We are closed until Tuesday. Please leave a—"

I hung up. I knew ultra-efficient Trish Laharne would phone me back, like she had before. But I'd changed my mind about leaving a message. I couldn't get Laharne or anyone else involved. It had to be me and Mike, face to face.

I was scheduled to play in the Keynote courtyard on British Columbia Day, holiday Monday. Mike wouldn't be there, though. He and Bo were going sailing. Tuesday would be my D-Day with him. D for him doing something about the townhouse people. Or D for me being a dunce, alienating him and getting fired.

Just as I reached the bus shelter I heard, "Nate!"

Zandi caught up to me.

"I've been yelling your name for three blocks." She leaned against the shelter to catch her breath.

Zandi, hop-running toward me? I'd have thought she'd choose the opposite direction, possibly into a different province.

"I was thinking about leaving a voicemail," I explained. "When you have low-voltage brain power, even the simplest task takes concentration."

One of her panted-out breaths turned into a laugh. I didn't get this girl. High-voltage contradictions from one minute to the next. She held up the Beethoven wig. "You forgot this! I tried calling you and got a message with you apologizing and asking if I'd give you another sneeze."

Ah, yes. The lemon outfit. I explained, "Some dust got in the way. It was another *chance* I was hoping you'd give me."

Zandi lifted her hands in a gesture of surrender. "That does it. I don't think of you as the enemy anymore, Crocker. You're too goofy to not trust."

"Thanks. I think. And, uh, sorry about the chip comment."

We grinned at each other, sat down on the bus-shelter seat.

Zandi heaved one more big breath and nodded. "Okay. Me-to-you download. The file wasn't paper. It wasn't about protesting or about meeting Robert Pattinson. It was an audio file on my phone. I'd recorded Mike Dante in the courtyard. He was laughing with Beethovens One, Two and Three. Saying people who get tossed out of aging rental buildings are nobodies, losers. Saying they aren't worth thinking about."

Holiday Monday. Visitors crammed the Keynote courtyard. Many waved the BC flag, with its big, radiant sun. Proud British Columbians. Or else they were fanning themselves. The real sun was blasting down, hottest yet this summer.

This time I was heat-ready. I had a spare T-shirt wrapped around my head to absorb sweat. After every tune I reached into my backpack for one of several water bottles. I glugged some of the water, then emptied the rest over my head.

The Fifth Beethoven

I finished up *Fifth Symphony* with my usual rip-the-knuckles-down-the-keys. The crowd offered up the usual cheers, claps and tips in my upturned cap.

But my grins and thank-yous were different. I was faking them. I was uncomfortable about having hot—yeah, I know, bad pun—property in my backpack. Until the Knox Costume Company reopened tomorrow, I was stuck with the accidentally stolen Beethoven outfit.

A woman tucked a ten into my cap and said, "That's some fifth Beethoven."

In spite of the intense heat, ice ran down my spine. How did the woman know I had the fifth costume?

The woman was viewing me with a puzzled frown. I replayed her words. *That's some fifth Beethoven*. Reset, Crocker. She'd been complimenting me. As in, *That's some Fifth, Beethoven*.

I managed a weak smile. "Wow, ma'am. Thanks! Calling me Beethoven. That means a lot. Though Ludwig's ghost is no doubt clenching his fists, ready to strike."

The woman laughed. I didn't. Because Ludwig's ghost was indeed standing beside her, clenching his fists. *Just a joke*, I mental-texted him.

He faded. Slowly, like he might change his mind. I started in on "Ode to Joy." I crashed my hands down on the keys the way I felt the world was crashing down on me. It wasn't just the stolen costume I was stressed about. It was the idea of confronting Mike. Did he know families waiting for apartments were sardined into narrow townhouses? Did he really view displaced renters as losers?

Mike didn't notice me listening, Zandi had explained. *I was sitting on the bench, waiting for the other protesters to show up. I'd forgotten my sign, so I looked like anybody else. Like a nobody, as Mike would put it. When he started insulting renters, this nobody switched on her recording app.*

I stopped playing. No matter how I felt, "Ode to Joy" deserved better than this. I took a deep breath and mentally apologized to Beethoven. I played the beginning over again, happy, *legato*. I sped it up. Best way to deal with a hot day: *sizzle* it.

I felt better. The crowd caught my mood, swayed and tapped their feet. One couple started jiving. They dipped, they spun; the man whirled the lady up high.

At the end cheers, whistles and stomping filled the courtyard. I stretched out my hand to the couple. The crowd cheered louder.

Break time. I took a swig of the last full bottle, poured the rest over my head. "Be back shortly," I promised. I headed to the Keynote.

"Hey Crocker, you forgot your money." It was Zandi, holding out the tip-crammed cap I'd left on top of the piano.

I grinned, pleased to see her. Somewhat surprised, too. I was pretty sure we'd moved past the enemies stage. But with Zandi you never knew.

"Come into the Keynote with me. I'm going to fill bottles at the water foun- tain. Plus, it's about eighty degrees cooler inside."

She gave the world's tallest quarter note

a dubious glance, then looked at the cap. "You should put this somewhere safe."

"I have a highly efficient, ultra-secure storage plan," I assured her. I took the cap, noticing a folded piece of paper on top. Wow, people were giving tips via *cheques* now? Opening my backpack, I took the cap and randomly dumped the contents inside.

That seemed to relax Zandi. Possibly she found stupidity soothing. We walked into the Keynote together. I rehydrated at the drinking fountain and refilled my bottles.

Zandi wandered around. She checked out the Beethoven portrait, then disappeared along the curving glass wall of the restaurant.

Cramming the bottles into my backpack, I followed. She was glaring at the Businessperson of the Year plaque.

"Yeah, I know," I said. "If Mike knows about the townhouses, this award makes no sense. And joking about renters being losers—I'd sure like to hear that audio file."

She turned away from the plaque.

High-beamed me with her dark, and at this moment angry, eyes. "Small hope of that. Constable Barker warned me not to expect my phone back. He said the thief would wipe it clean and sell it. I didn't want to believe him. The audio recording was a chance, finally, for me to confront Mike. To shame him into treating us renovicted tenants better."

I didn't say anything. I was imagining Mom and me getting renovicted. Which, in develop-first, think-later Vancouver, could easily happen. I realized I was becoming like Mom, thinking about that more and more.

Zandi must have seen bitterness in my face. She managed a smile. "I should stop obsessing about the file. Unhealthy, right? Problem is, I also miss the phone. It was navy blue, streaked with silver. Classy. Unlike…" She pulled the glittery pink phone from her pocket, sighed, put it back again.

Glitter, I thought. *Glittery phones— and glittery watches*. I looked around. I'd thought the lobby seemed quiet. No wonder. The security guard wasn't here.

I checked the reception desk. Sladen might be in Bo Dante mode, reclining in his chair and sleeping. I leaned over the counter. Nope.

Zandi joined me. I pointed to the large, open bag of pistachio nuts. "Our burly friend is here but goofing off. With the boss away I guess he's not worried about staying on duty."

She surveyed the shells littering the counter. "Not worried about being a slob, either."

"He's into attacking food," I explained. "The guy opens his pistachios with a hammer."

Zandi laughed. "With a hammer? That's wild."

Bells tinkled. She lifted her phone. "Hi Mom...I'm at the Keynote, hanging out with my friend Nate. I told you about him. The pianist who rocks Beethoven."

My friend. Wow. Definitely past the enemy stage. I felt good about that.

Then I felt something else: my foot crushing a pistachio shell. I replayed Zandi's comment. Cracking nuts with a hammer was wild, all right. Maybe too wild. The counter was high enough that I hadn't actually seen hammer meet pistachio.

I rushed around the other side of the counter. Reaching both hands wide, I brushed shells toward the middle. I noticed a stack of golf magazines, also thick with shells. I shook every magazine out.

With Tiger Woods I hit the jackpot. A magazine with the golf legend's smiling face on the cover spilled out shells—

And one navy and silver-streaked fragment of metal.

I let loose a swear word.

Zandi covered her phone. "Do you *mind*? My mom heard that!"

I gaped at her, unable to speak. I was in shock. Shell shock.

I held the piece of metal out to Zandi. "It wasn't pistachios the guard was smashing. It was your old phone."

Her new phone erupted: "Zandi, are you all right? Who's swearing at you?"

I leaned over, spoke into the phone.

"This is Nate Crocker, ma'am. Sorry about the swearing. I'm having a bad reaction to some pistachios."

Zandi's mom gasped. "Are you having trouble breathing? Tell me exactly where you are. I'll call for an ambulance."

Zandi took the phone. "It's fine, Mom. I'll explain later."

She clicked off, took the metal fragment from me. Studied it. "Why would the guard smash a perfectly good phone? Selling it would make more sense."

"Not if," I said slowly, "there was something on the phone he wanted to destroy."

Zandi paused, took that in. Her dark eyes widened. "My recording of Mike."

I didn't want to answer. I got a bottle from my backpack. Chugged back some water. But I couldn't stall my reply—or my thoughts—forever.

"Yeah," I said at last. "The guard wouldn't have cared about the file himself. But his boss would. If Mike's comments about renters were as bad as you say, Mike would want the file destroyed."

I expected Zandi to get angry.

She didn't. Like I say, a girl of surprises. Her gaze turned sympathetic. "Bummer. I know you like Mike Dante, look up to him."

I did look up to Mike. Since I met him things had looked up for me. Except there was no up now.

"I was right about the thief going for three thefts as cover for one," I said. "But I got the target wrong. It wasn't the ruby earrings he was after. It was your phone."

Chapter Sixteen

Zandi turned the metal fragment sideways. Silver flashed against navy. Sounding dazed, she murmured, "I liked this design. It reminded me of my favourite painting, Van Gogh's *Starry Night*. So clever the way Van Gogh turned the sky into swirls of movement."

Van Gogh sounded cool. But I needed to get Zandi Van Gone from the topic. "Let's try to figure this out. When the fourth Beethoven grabbed your bag, you were going into the Keynote. You had an appointment with Mike."

She nodded. "I was angry. I planned to play him the recording, show him I knew he didn't really care about people."

"Who knew you had the recording?"

"The other protesters. I played it for them, then phoned Mike's office. I told his assistant, Ms. Laharne, that I had to talk to Mr. Dante about something important. I didn't say what. She gave me an appointment right away."

I thought about Ms. Laharne taking calls. So many people anxious to meet with Mike, get what they could out of him. VIPs like the mayor, she'd oblige. But a renovicted teenager?

I thought some more. I liked Trish Laharne. Sure, she had a strange laugh, but what were a few whinnies between friends? *No. Put the friends thing aside, Crocker*, I thought. Laharne being nice was ambient noise, a distraction.

I tapped the water bottle against the counter, bah-bah-bah-*boom*. I had it. I didn't like it, but I had it. "There was never going to be an appointment. Laharne knew about the recording."

Again I remembered what Mike had said about Laharne that first day: *She takes care of everything.* She'd taken care of this, too.

Maybe, I thought hopefully, *Mike hadn't even been aware of it.*

Zandi went over to the window and gazed out. "But who told Laharne? It couldn't have been a protester. Mike Dante renovicted them, too. They wouldn't want to help him."

I joined her at the window. It was so hot people were ignoring the *Do not wade in the fountain* sign. They were laughing and splashing each other.

"Where did you play the recording?" I asked.

"On the bench where we always sit. The one near the vendor." She stared across to the news kiosk. A few people were reading magazines. Or pretending to, while they enjoyed the shade from the kiosk's roof.

Zandi and I looked at each other. That was it. Someone pretending to read by the kiosk had listened in.

"Laharne," I said. "Later, when she got your call, her take-care-of-everything brain came up with Operation Phone Destroy. She ordered Sladen to quick-change into the fourth Beethoven costume—and attack."

Zandi shuddered. "We should go to Constable Barker."

"Yeah. But first I'll talk to Mike, show him the special-size costume order. Explain that Sladen wore it—but not to fill in for one of the other Beethovens."

Zandi put the metal phone fragment back in my palm. "Show Mike this, too. I wish I could be there. But Mike is more likely to talk if it's just you. He likes you, Nate. Whatever else about him is phony, that isn't."

Yeah. That was what made confronting him so tough.

I rested my forehead against the window. Outside, chomping on a burger, Sladen marched up to the splashers. Yelled at them with his mouth full. They scattered. I imagined him subbing for a regular Beethoven. Growling where the others made jokes. As long as he didn't say anything he'd be okay.

"Huh," I commented.

"You're thinking," Zandi said. "That's never good."

Pushing rhododendrons aside, I knocked on the Shermans' door. I hoped Mallory would answer. Not the fierce, fist-clenching husband.

The door opened and—

It was him. He already had his fist raised.

I pretended not to notice that the guy looked ready to punch me. "I'm here because parents want me to entertain at kids' birthday parties. I may be out of a job soon, so I was hoping to get names from Mallory."

The man kept his upraised hand clenched. With his other hand he reached for my elbow and drew me inside.

The house was quiet. Which meant no witnesses. The perfect moment to pummel the daylights out of me. I lifted my eyes to his upraised fist, saw what he was holding.

A baton.

I looked past him to the photo on the piano. The sun shone on the glass like it had before. This time, squinting, I made out the baton.

I saw something else in the living room: a lectern with sheet music and headphones on it.

"You're a conductor," I said weakly.

His smile relaxed his face, turned him non-fierce. "I was practising for tonight's concert. I'm assistant conductor with the Vancouver Symphony Orchestra." He held out his hand. "Gerald Sherman. And you're the talented, funny Nate Crocker. Thanks to you, my son Randall is bashing away at his piano every day."

I shook his hand. Phew! Talk about having the wrong idea about someone.

But it wasn't only relief I felt. Randall was sticking with his music. That made me feel good. A quiet, pleased good, I realized, as opposed to flashy, look-at-me-impressing-Mike-Dante good.

Gerald was saying, "I tried for months to get Randall interested. All I got was—"

I said it with him: "Nobody can make me."

We laughed. He led me into the living room. He sprawled in a chair. "I'll give you parents' names. But I've been wanting to talk to you about something else: lessons."

I sat on the edge of the sofa. I cleared my throat. "I'm flattered, sir. But I'm not qualified to teach Randall. I don't have any fancy conservatory training."

"Not lessons for Randall. For *you*. I'm starting a young musicians' program for the symphony. I'm looking for young people with raw talent. Kids who haven't had the resources for lessons." Gerald sat forward and spoke earnestly. "It would be an opportunity for you to build on what you already know. On the natural gift you have."

"Bah-bah-bah-*boom*," I breathed.

Gerald grinned. Then he looked puzzled. "The other day I heard you playing through the window. I tried to talk to you about this. But you ran away. Like you were scared."

Oh, man. This was a misunderstanding I did *not* want to explain. I could say one thing with complete truth: "Sorry. Work's been a bummer."

Gerald rolled his eyes. "Ah yes, your boss. Mike 'I'm everybody's friend' Dante. That guy never met a money-making scheme he didn't like. Never mind about Dante. He sucks up enough of our city's oxygen as it is. If he lets you go, it's his loss." He grinned. "Much more important: Are you interested in taking lessons at the symphony?"

I gulped. I thought of the doom-filled faces of kids going to Mrs. Snythe's. I'd always felt superior. Felt so sure I could make it without lessons.

"I'll make the lessons fun," Gerald promised. "Fair warning, though: I'll also make them challenging. I'll want you to achieve more than you think you can. Because I *know* you can."

I liked the sound of that. But I couldn't think. I was too stressed about meeting Mike.

I said, "I appreciate this, sir. Er, maestro. I'll let you know."

Chapter Seventeen

When I stepped out of the elevator, Mike's assistant was hunched over her computer. She was frowning and pushing her straw-blonde bangs out of her eyes.

"Good morning, Ms. Laharne," I greeted her. "I…"

Beethoven sauntered up beside me, yawning under his mask. I continued. "Er, Bo and I are here to see Mike."

Laharne shot us a stressed smile. "Sorry, can't talk now. Busy. Quarterly reports."

Unlike Laharne, Mike was smiling at his computer screen. On seeing me he smiled even wider.

I said, "Sir, there's something I need to talk to you about."

Bo started to lift his hand in a hello gesture to his dad. The effort was apparently too much for him. Letting his hand flop, he made for the sofa. Stretched out. Naptime.

I wondered what Mike thought about this. Even for Sleeping Bo-ty, snoozing first thing in the morning was odd. But Mike ignored Bo. He gushed, "You are the best, Nate Crocker. The. Best."

He turned his computer screen to me. I saw myself, frozen in mid-jump behind the courtyard piano. Mike clicked the play arrow.

It was yesterday's performance. Somebody had posted a vidoe of me bashing out "Ode To Joy" on YouTube. After a few moments the shot switched to the couple jiving.

I'd never seen Mike's blue eyes so bright, so pleased. "Nine thousand views and counting. You're like me. You like pleasing crowds. You're a born entertainer."

I listened to my playing. Maybe it was seeing Gerald Sherman yesterday, his talking about challenging me to improve. I heard the exuberance in my performance. But I also heard the flaws.

"So. Tell me what you wanted to talk about," Mike invited.

I pulled out the phone fragment and the Knox customer order for a special-size costume. I placed them on Mike's desk. Told him about Zandi's phone recording. About suspecting Laharne had ordered the guard to steal it. And about the guard's worth-its-weight-in-rubies watch.

All I got was a blue-eyed stare. I'd offended Mike. Of course I had. What did I expect, claiming two of his employees were criminals?

Then Mike's face softened. "You're a conscientious kid. You had an idea about the robberies and followed it through. That took energy. And you do have energy." He chuckled. "My advice? Save the energy for your music. Leave cop stuff to the cops."

"B-but this evidence," I stammered.

Mike laced his fingers together, rested his chin on them. Smiled. "At the time of the three robberies in the Keynote courtyard, the security guard—Pruitt—was with Bo and his two friends at a pizza lunch. There are witnesses. Ask Constable Barker."

"Pruitt," I repeated stupidly. "I thought his name was Sladen. Pruitt sounds like a butler."

He laughed. "Full name: Pruitt Sladen. He hates his first name, so for a joke that's what I call him. Anyhow, Pruitt, Sladen, whatever. His alibi is rock-solid."

I wouldn't have minded a rock myself. To crawl under. "I don't know how I got it so wrong, sir. I'm sorry."

Mike sat back. "Not to worry. As for this phone recording, if your friend heard me making fun of renters, well, as you know I do joke around a lot. I didn't mean to insult anyone."

"They're sardined into townhouses," I blurted.

Mike's face grew serious. "I know. We underestimated the number of people who'd need housing. Trust me, Nate. I'm on it."

Slowly I nodded. He'd made a mistake. Mistakes were human. Look at me. I'd just made a whopper.

I glanced at Mike's computer screen, at the video paused on the man whirling the woman high in the air. 9K views and counting.

Mike got up, walked around the desk, gave my shoulder a friendly squeeze. "You're just not cut out to be a cop. Let me get you a bracing cup of joe. You look like you need it." He strolled over to the espresso machine, pushed the button.

I couldn't believe it. I'd screwed up and he was being nice to me.

The machine made chugging noises. I watched the liquid ooze into a cup. I'd have to down it. After all, he was being nice. *You're just not meant to be a cop.*

Obviously he was right. Except that—

Except that Constable Barker had said the opposite. *You have the two main qualifications. You want to help people and you like doughnuts.* Wouldn't a cop have—well, a cop's instinct about such things?

The Fifth Beethoven

I massaged my shoulder. Mike had intended the squeeze to be reassuring. Unfortunately this was the shoulder Sladen—Pruitt—had crunched. It was still tender. Not that Mike could have known that. He was being nice.

Mike held out the cup of vile, I mean, gourmet espresso. I took it and thanked him. Then glanced around. That nearby potted plant: perfect.

"Could I see more of the video?" I asked.

Mike returned to his computer, pressed the spacebar. "Hey! We're almost at ten thousand views," he exclaimed.

I emptied the cup into the soil. Hoped the plant wouldn't wither and die. Joined Mike in watching the video.

The camera stayed on the jiving couple for another minute. Then it swung to— Randall Sherman! I hadn't known he was there. Behind him, clapping to the music, were Mallory and Gerald. Cool.

As usual, Randall was doing the windmill thing, wildly waving his arms. When music got going, the kid got elastic. I loved it.

Mike punched the spacebar, *stop*. "We can use this video for promotion, but we'll have to edit out the gimpy kid."

Gimpy, I thought. No. Mike couldn't have said that. "But the crowd loves him."

By way of reply Mike flailed his arms, twisted his body, stuck his tongue out and rolled his eyes.

Then he laughed heartily. "That's just it, Crocker. The little gimp flapping around distracts from you. We don't want weird at the Keynote. We want rockin', sockin', wholesome, normal-people entertainment."

Gimp. He'd said it again. A revolting, insulting word. My brain fought back, told me I'd misheard. Yeah, that was it. Constant loud music had damaged my hearing.

Mike chuckled. "I got nothing against freaks, Crocker. There are homes for them, right? But not at the Keynote. I mean, I have image to think about. No place for freaks at the Keynote. I start putting gimpy kids in our promotions, and the next thing you know the place will be crawling with every half-wit and weirdo in the city."

Randall. A freak. A gimp. My brain went MIA. I couldn't think.

Mike beamed at me. "Now *you*, Crocker. You're great for the Dante Enterprises image. You and I are putting show biz into the real estate biz. We should think about adding you into my commercials. Like that idea?"

"Sure. Yeah." I made myself smile. I should be thrilled. But I couldn't feel anything. Randall. A gimp.

Mike clapped me on the back. "So we're okay? You'll leave the cop work to Barker?"

I nodded, robot-like.

"Super. Now off to work with you. Your fans are waiting. Go out there and rock 'em up to the stratosphere."

"Yes, sir. I mean, yes, Mike." I started walking out of the office.

"Yo, Bo," Mike called over to the sofa. "Wake up. Trish has our morning bagels on the way."

Bo got up, slowly, leisurely. Placing his phone against his ear, he raised a forefinger in a just-a-minute gesture. He listened and nodded into the phone. He followed me out of the office.

I wondered if Mike thought it strange, his son wearing the Beethoven mask up here in the office.

And I hoped, really hoped, Mike didn't notice the colour of the phone Bo was clutching.

Glittery pink.

Chapter Eighteen

Trish Laharne was still squinting at her screen. Bo—I mean, the fifth Beethoven—I mean, Zandi—and I sprinted for the elevator. Twenty yards...ten...

The elevator doors slid open. The real Bo Dante, mask and wig tucked under one arm, sauntered out.

Zandi veered into the conference room and shut the door—on a silky flap of shirt hem. She had to open the door to free it.

I thought Bo might notice. But our night sailor was in mid-yawn.

From his office Mike called, "Bo! You want bagels or not?"

Bo finished his yawn, blinked to wake himself up more. "Sure, Dad. Why wouldn't I?"

"Bagels!" squealed Laharne as she pressed her hands against the sides of her head. "This horrid report—*I forgot the bagels.*" She jabbed a speed-dial number and rattled off an order for bagels, cream cheese and blackberry jam.

This would have made me hungry if I hadn't been crazy nervous. What if a meeting was scheduled for the conference room? What if someone walked in on the fifth Beethoven?

I stepped in front of the conference room door. Tried to look casual.

Laharne glanced up, gave a harried smile. "You're welcome to bagels, too, Nate. I order lots."

I thought of all the times Laharne been nice to me. Arranging use of the Keynote grand piano. Leaving snacks every day. This same person had dreamed up the thefts in the courtyard. A nice person— with a fang-sharp mind. *Get back to your reports, Trish*, I mentally urged her. *Don't notice me loitering.*

"I'm fine, thanks, Ms. Laharne. Just, uh,"

The Fifth Beethoven

I slipped my backpack off and opened it, "making sure I have my sheet music."

She nodded and resumed staring at her screen. I made a show of scrabbling around in the backpack. With a sigh of relief I drew out my sheet music—also some of the bills and coins I'd dumped in yesterday. Plus that folded piece of paper. That cheque.

I let everything else fall back in. It wasn't a cheque. It was a sketch of a girl, with the initials ZS in a corner. Slowly I grinned, getting it. The girl was Zandi. She was on top of the Keynote, dropping a huge potato chip off the edge.

A chip. The chip on her shoulder about me. She was letting it go.

When she'd handed me my cap and tip money she'd tucked the sketch in. No wonder she wanted to make sure I didn't lose the cap.

Behind me Zandi quietly opened the door. She was back to her usual shorts and *Give Us Back Our Homes!* T-shirt. She had the Beethoven costume bundled up under one arm.

Laharne didn't glance over. Too preoccupied. I held up the sketch. Zandi shook her head in exasperation. "Took you long enough to find it."

I grinned wider. "So maybe we might grab a burger sometime? Chat like regular, non-hostile people?"

"Nope."

"Oh. Okay, then."

Her dark eyes twinkled. "No burger for me. I'm more of a pizza kind of girl."

She handed me the Beethoven costume. Busy grinning, I stuffed it into my backpack without looking. When I tried to zip it shut, part of the wig stuck out, trapped in the zipper.

By now we had caught Laharne's attention. She was frowning at the black wig hairs jutting out of the backpack. I could almost hear her fang-sharp brain snapping to attention.

"Oh, these?" I said, with an airy laugh. "Just cobwebs. I need to clean my backpack out more often. You know what they say: cleanliness is next to godliness."

Like I, *I*, would ever quote that. Zandi and I bolted for the elevator.

Panic-punching the close-doors button, Zandi didn't look back down the hall. But I did. I saw Mike's assistant, still with that frown, hunch over her computer screen again. I heard her frustrated sigh.

And I both saw and heard Laharne raise her hands, close the right over the left and squeeze. *Pop! Pop! Pop!*

The elevator sped down. It took several floors before I managed to choke out, "The special-order size. Not extra-large. Extra *small*. Trish Laharne was the thief."

"Trish?" Zandi gasped. The *sshh* of the doors opening into the lobby seemed to echo the name.

We walked past Pruitt Sladen. He was leafing through a golf magazine. I barely saw him. I was remembering Laharne by the elevator with Mike. Saying, *Martha Shulman is stuck at the Hong Kong airport.*

Won't be able to make tomorrow's meeting. No worries, boss. Martha will send her notes to me. I'll fill in for her.

Because Laharne took care of every-thing—and that included subbing for other employees. I'd assumed the fourth costume was for Sladen. If one of the other Beethovens couldn't come in, he'd wear it. I'd had it wrong. Not Sladen. Laharne.

In the courtyard Zandi glanced doubtfully at her phone. "Speaking of Beethovens, I'm not sure how successful I was as the fifth. I recorded Mike but didn't get anything we can use. He didn't diss renters."

"He was too busy dissing Randall," I said bitterly.

"That was horrible," Zandi agreed. "So much for the Dante image. Imagine if people heard that."

We looked at each other. "Imagine," I said.

Zandi gulped. "It would shame him, all right. To make himself look good again, he might actually do something nice, like finding homes for those of us squashed into townhouses. But we can't go public. People might figure out who the kid in the video is. We can't do that to Randall and his family."

A gimp. No, we couldn't.

"We tried, Crocker," Zandi sounded more sad than angry. She headed off to the protesters' bench.

I set my music on the piano rack.

Then the encore act: Ludwig appeared on the other side of the piano.

This ghost thing is getting old, I thought-messaged him.

He scowled. I scowled back. *What do you want? We tried. We got nothing.*

The composer brandished some rolled-up music sheets. Peeling off the dedication page, he tore it in two.

He disappeared. I gaped after him, bewildered. Ghost Beethoven had just recreated his temper tantrum about Napoleon. He'd ripped up the first part of his music. What was the point of that?

Wait. *The first part*, I thought.

I ran, caught up with Zandi. "Mike

insulted the kid in the video: true. People might figure out the kid was Randall: also true. *But Mike only did that in the first part of his remarks.* After that, he was ranting about any kid who acted weird. About how he wouldn't want to attract them to the Keynote."

"You're right," Zandi said slowly. "If we cut that first part out…"

"We could use the rest."

She nodded. She looked like I felt. Scared. "But who would we play it for?"

"I don't know. Constable Barker, maybe. Or city council." I rubbed my forehead, trying to activate my brain. "I'm more idea than plan at this point. Let's talk about it on my break."

"Maybe we start with a parent," Zandi suggested. "Parents are generally sensible."

She went join her buddies. I jogged back to the piano. *Sensible*, I thought.

The Fifth Beethoven

The crowd was the biggest ever. *Must be the YouTube video*, I thought. I plugged the portable speaker into the piano. For the first time I might need it.

Time to rock out the *Fifth*. I poised my fingers over the keys—

And didn't play. I had the fourth, not the *Fifth*, in my mind. The fourth Beethoven. Trish Laharne.

Did Mike know Laharne was the thief? Again I wanted, so wanted, to believe Laharne acted on her own. Right after Zandi phoned, the whinnying assistant had donned her Beethoven duds and headed out. That didn't exactly leave time for a consultation with Mike.

Ba-ba-ba-*boom!* I started in on the *Fifth*. I would talk to Constable Barker, give him the evidence. His problem now. No more thinking for me. Thinking was painful. Thinking took you places you might not like.

I played one tune after another, never stopping, straight through to break. The crowd loved it. They danced, cheered, clapped. So many of them today.

And then I did have a thought. Zandi and I had wondered which person to play the recording for: Constable Barker, a city councillor, a parent.

The crowd was whistling, whooping their appreciation. So many of them today. So many people.

After my break the courtyard filled with noise again. Not my noise. Oh, I was back at the piano. Just not playing.

Mike was providing the sound. From the protesters' bench his voice blasted:

"I got nothing against freaks, Crocker. There are homes for them, right? But not at the Keynote. I mean, I have *image* to think about…"

The crowd was completely transfixed by the recording Zandi was playing. Some people, probably visitors, looked puzzled. The locals recognized Mike Dante's voice.

"No place for freaks at the Keynote. I start putting gimpy kids in our promotions, and the next thing you know the place will be crawling with every half-wit and weirdo in the city."

The Keynote's revolving doors spun. Mike bounded over to me, his blue eyes out-blazing the sun. "That Beethoven in my office earlier. It wasn't Bo. It was one of those protesters in disguise. Recorded me, can you believe it? I've called my lawyer. No worries, Crocker. We'll shut them down."

He didn't suspect me. He still trusted me. That was the gut punch. *He still trusted me.*

Mike took in the sight of me not playing. His gaze turned puzzled. "What happened to your portable speaker?" he asked. He didn't wait for my answer. Good thing, because I'd given it to Zandi during break. "Never mind, doesn't matter. You're Rocker Crocker. You can out-volume them without a speaker. Do it!"

He was smiling, hopeful. I was his guy.

A TV news van was pulling up. A woman brandishing a mic jumped out, followed by a man with a video camera. They shoved through the crowd to the protesters.

Mike exclaimed, "What the—"

It could be me they'd hurry toward. If I played. Because a lot of my playing was about volume. That's why Mike gave me this opportunity, I saw that now. He wanted me to drown out the protesters. To drown out any hint that he wasn't a cheerful, welcoming, all-round good corporate citizen.

Except he wasn't welcoming to everyone. That was clear from the comments that boomed out:

"No place for freaks at the Keynote. I mean, I have *image* to think about!"

Mike watched me, a slight frown forming. But he was still smiling, still confident about me.

I thought of Beethoven ripping up the page of music dedicated to Napoleon. Like I'd told Randall, some of the best music was about defiance.

I looked at Mike. I didn't play. It practically killed me not to.

But I didn't play.

Coda

The vendor thumped down the morning papers. He glanced at the headline: *Dante apologizes for 'gimpy kid' comments, promises to find homes for displaced tenants.*

The vendor reached for his morning coffee, took several creamy, sugary slurps. With coffee he could face anything. Even the knuckle-cracker.

Come to think of it, the vendor hadn't seen her for a while. Or that burly dude who bought golf magazines.

It was early. The only person nearby was the piano-playing kid sitting on a bench. The vendor didn't approve of the kid. He played too loud. And that hair! Anyone with hair that untidy would never amount to anything.

But today the vendor felt sorry for the kid. He looked unhappy. The vendor hadn't seen him around for a while. Not since that huge crowd, the noise, the TV cameras.

The kid's phone blared out several notes. The what's-it symphony. The vendor nodded, pleased with himself for (sort of) recognizing it.

The kid winced, held the phone away from his head. "Hold on, Ches," he said. He punched a button.

The voice of Ches—what kind of name was *that*?—blasted into the courtyard. "Hey. So, Nate. Just wanted to tell you I regifted that pen. It was Mom's birthday."

The kid, Nate, brightened. *Talking to Checkers, or whatever his friend's name is, cheers him up*, the vendor thought.

Nate said, "Good to hear from you. That's cool about the pen. Did your mom like it?"

"Mega-liked it. She said it was nice of me to give her something so elegant. Go figure, huh? I mean, a *pen*." The blasting voice hesitated for a moment. "Uh. I hear you're not working for Dante Enterprises anymore."

The kid's shoulders slumped. "I'm not, no. That's over. I'll be getting into entertaining at birthday parties for the kindergarten set."

"What?!" Owl-like hoots blasted around the courtyard, startling the vendor into spilling some coffee.

Nate continued, "Yeah, really. And I was thinking. I've been doing a lot of thinking the past few days. I had the idea that eventually you and I could partner up on birthday parties. I provide the music, you provide the food."

"Huh." The loud voice sounded thoughtful.

"It's just in the dream stage for now," Nate said quickly. "Dreams don't always work out, but you never know."

"Huh. Yeah."

Crisp footsteps sounded on the courtyard tiles. A cop was heading Nate's way.

"Gotta go, Ches. We'll talk. Soon, okay?" The kid crammed his phone into a pocket. He stood up. "Hey, Constable."

He and the police officer started talking.

The kid got his sad expression again. At one point the constable patted the kid's arm, like he was comforting him.

The vendor was curious. That is to say, with no customers yet, he had nothing else to occupy him. He slurped his coffee and edged closer. Looked down, pretended to read the newspaper, the always-bad news.

The cop was saying, "Sladen got scared and talked. Admitted Laharne gave him the stuff she'd stolen. She said he could have it all, including the rubies, if he destroyed the phone."

The kid started to speak, hesitated. Finally blurted, "And Mike? Did he know?"

"When we confronted her, Laharne took full responsibility. Said Dante wasn't involved."

Nate said nothing. Looked kind of sad, the vendor thought.

The cop opened a box of doughnuts, held it out. "Here. Chocolate-glazed, walnut-sprinkled. And Crocker? There are such things as musical cops."

The kid didn't take one. The vendor

didn't get that. His own mouth was watering like Niagara Falls. He decided to crack open his lunchbox, get an early start on his sandwich.

The vendor didn't pay attention to what else the kid and the cop said just then. He was too busy swooning as he unwrapped his food. Peanut butter and pickle, heavy on both. His favourite. He sank his teeth in and eavesdropped again.

"I texted Gerald Sherman," the kid was saying. "Told him if his offer was still open, I'd take it."

"Excellent. And what did Sherman say?"

The kid stopped looking sad. Finally, *finally*, took a doughnut. Grinned. "He texted back, 'Bah-bah-bah-*boom*.'"

Acknowledgements

As a crescendo, thank you to my editor and publisher Melanie Jeffs, for working on me with this story, encouraging me and including me in the wonderful new adventure that is Crwth Press. Thanks also to Renée Layberry for her eagle-eyed editing!

About
Melanie Jackson

Like her protagonist Nate, Melanie Jackson plays piano with more enthusiasm than training. As for the character of Randall, who is on the autism spectrum, she modelled him partly after her brother. Melanie has written numerous books for young people and is busy plotting a new one. Melanie lives in Vancouver, British Columbia. Follow her @melaniejackson or visit melaniejacksonblog.wordpress.com.

About Crwth Press

Crwth (pronounced crooth) Press is a small independent publisher based in British Columbia. A crwth is a Welsh stringed instrument that was commonly played in Wales until the mid-1800s, when it was replaced by the violin. We chose this word for the company name because we like the way music brings people together, and we want our press to do the same.

Crwth Press is committed to sustainability and accessibility. This book is printed in Canada on 100 percent post-consumer waste paper using only vegetable-based inks. For more on our sustainability model, visit www.crwth.ca.

To make our books accessible, we use fonts that individuals with dyslexia find easier to read. The font for this book is Lexie Readable.